A SHOOTING STAR

'I will not be defeated so easily,' she told herself. 'Even if they win, I am certain I will find a way to escape.'

Flavia went over to the window and pulled back the curtains.

When she looked out, the moon was just appearing in the darkening sky and the first star was twinkling near it.

She stood looking up at them, feeling that in some way they might help her.

Then suddenly a shooting star sped across the sky and disappeared behind the roofs of the houses.

It was almost as if the Heavens had spoken to her.

The shooting star told her there was always a way out, however frightening the future might seem.

Like the shooting star, she would somehow evade them and they would be unable to catch her.

'That is what I wanted to know,' she determined.

She threw back her head and looked up at the sky again.

"Thank you," she whispered. "Now I know that you are with me and I am no longer alone."

THE BARBARA CARTLAND PINK COLLECTION

Titles in this series

A SHOOTING STAR

BARBARA CARTLAND

Barbaracartland.com Ltd

THE BARBARA CARTLAND PINK COLLECTION

Dame Barbara Cartland is still regarded as the most prolific bestselling author in the history of the world.

In her lifetime she was frequently in the Guinness Book of Records for writing more books than any other living author.

Her most amazing literary feat was to double her output from 10 books a year to over 20 books a year when she was 77 to meet the huge demand.

She went on writing continuously at this rate for 20 years and wrote her very last book at the age of 97, thus completing an incredible 400 books between the ages of 77 and 97.

Her publishers finally could not keep up with this phenomenal output, so at her death in 2000 she left behind an amazing 160 unpublished manuscripts, something that no other author has ever achieved.

Barbara's son, Ian McCorquodale, together with his daughter Iona, felt that it was their sacred duty to publish all these titles for Barbara's millions of admirers all over the world who so love her wonderful romances.

So in 2004 they started publishing the 160 brand new Barbara Cartlands as *The Barbara Cartland Pink Collection*, as Barbara's favourite colour was always pink – and yet more pink!

The Barbara Cartland Pink Collection is published monthly exclusively by Barbaracartland.com and the books are numbered in sequence from 1 to 160.

Enjoy receiving a brand new Barbara Cartland book each month by taking out an annual subscription to the Pink Collection, or purchase the books individually.

The Pink Collection is available from the Barbara Cartland website www.barbaracartland.com via mail order and through all good bookshops.

In addition Ian and Iona are proud to announce that The Barbara Cartland Pink Collection is now available in ebook format as from Valentine's Day 2011.

For more information, please contact us at:

Barbaracartland.com Ltd.
Camfield Place
Hatfield
Hertfordshire AL9 6JE
United Kingdom

Telephone: +44 (0)1707 642629
Fax: +44 (0)1707 663041
Email: info@barbaracartland.com

THE LATE DAME BARBARA CARTLAND

Barbara Cartland who sadly died in May 2000 at the age of nearly 99 was the world's most famous romantic novelist who wrote 723 books in her lifetime with worldwide sales of over 1 billion copies and her books were translated into 36 different languages.

As well as romantic novels, she wrote historical biographies, 6 autobiographies, theatrical plays, books of advice on life, love, vitamins and cookery. She also found time to be a political speaker and television and radio personality.

She wrote her first book at the age of 21 and this was called *Jigsaw*. It became an immediate bestseller and sold 100,000 copies in hardback and was translated into 6 different languages. She wrote continuously throughout her life, writing bestsellers for an astonishing 76 years. Her books have always been immensely popular in the United States, where in 1976 her current books were at numbers 1 & 2 in the B. Dalton bestsellers list, a feat never achieved before or since by any author.

Barbara Cartland became a legend in her own lifetime and will be best remembered for her wonderful romantic novels, so loved by her millions of readers throughout the world.

Her books will always be treasured for their moral message, her pure and innocent heroines, her good looking and dashing heroes and above all her belief that the power of love is more important than anything else in everyone's life.

"I have often scanned the sky at night for a shooting star to bring me luck. Sometimes it works, sometimes it doesn't, but when a shooting star brings you love, then it is a very special star indeed."

Barbara Cartland

CHAPTER ONE
1878

Flavia Linwood gazed dreamily out of the window at the garden and thought she had never seen it look better.

There were flowers everywhere.

After a very cold and wet spring, the temperature had risen with the result that the flowers had bloomed and the weeds had flourished too.

Suddenly the whole place seemed to be transformed from the time of the long winter days.

Flavia loved being in the country and she was sad in some ways that she must now go to London.

Yet she knew that she would enjoy the endless balls and meeting her father's friends.

Her father had been saying for some time that she must 'come out' in a traditional Season, as it was only the mourning after her mother's death that had prevented her from being a *debutante* the previous year.

Queen Victoria had made the period of mourning of great Social significance and very lengthy – people were afraid to enjoy themselves if there had been a death in the family and they were to be dressed at all times in black.

Flavia, however, was thinking that most of all she would miss the horses she rode every morning, as well as swimming in the lake at the end of the garden, which she had done this ever since she was a child and some people thought this very strange on the part of a young girl.

But London was waiting for her.

When the maid came in to call her, she told her that the carriage had been ordered for nine-thirty.

"I'll have to hurry, Betsy," Flavia exclaimed. "As Papa will be annoyed if I arrive later than he expects."

"We'll miss you, Miss Flavia," the maid muttered. "But it be real right and proper for you to 'ave your time in London. It ought to 'ave been last year, but for your dear mother's passin' – God rest 'er soul."

Flavia did not answer and after she had washed, she dressed quickly.

She dressed in her very smart clothes that had been bought especially for her to travel to London.

One of her many aunts flattered herself that she had good taste and had gone to the most expensive shops in Bond Street for Flavia's 'coming out' wardrobe.

She was nearly nineteen and almost too old to be a *debutante*.

But, as she had not been able to appear at any of the balls last year, she was going to make up for it now.

She certainly looked extremely smart and elegant in a blue dress that reminded her of the forget-me-nots in the garden and she wore a hat to match trimmed with flowers.

"You look so lovely, Miss Flavia, you do really," Betsy sighed, "and we'll miss you till you be back with us again."

Flavia smiled at Betsy, who had looked after her ever since she had given up having a nanny.

"I'll miss you all at The Priory too, but don't forget we will come back whenever Papa is free and at least I will be home at the end of the summer."

Downstairs her breakfast was waiting for her and, as she finished eating, she heard the family carriage drawn by two fine horses coming round to the front door.

Her trunks were piled onto the top of the carriage and fastened to the back.

When she was finally ready to depart, the servants all came crowding into the hall to say goodbye to her.

There was the housekeeper, Mrs. Nelson, who ruled upstairs with a rod of iron.

There was their dependable cook, Mrs. Ruck, who had reigned supreme in the kitchen for over twenty years.

There was the old butler, Parkinson, who had given her sweetmeats in the pantry when she was old enough to toddle in to see him.

There were housemaids and scullions, footmen and nightwatchmen, all to see her off.

Flavia shook hands with each one of them and then Parkinson helped her into the carriage.

The senior housemaid, who was travelling with her followed closely behind.

As the horses started to move, there were cries of,

"Good luck, miss! Come home soon!"

Then they were driving down the long avenue of oak trees towards the lodge gates.

"I hate leaving home," Flavia said more to herself than to Martha, the housemaid.

"We'll all miss you," remarked Martha, "but, Miss Flavia, you mustn't forget the 'ouse in Grosvenor Square also be your 'ome."

"That is what Papa says, but I have been there so seldom that I can hardly remember what it's like."

"You'll soon remember, miss, once you're there, and I expects when it's time for you to return 'ome to The Priory, you'll be feelin' the other way round."

"I think that's very unlikely," said Flavia. "What I mind more than anything else is leaving the horses."

"You'll be ridin' in Rotten Row in London, miss, and very smart it be too from what I 'ears."

"I cannot believe it is as much fun as galloping over the fields and riding through the woods," Flavia insisted.

Martha did not answer and Flavia stared out of the window at the passing countryside.

It would take only three hours to reach London.

She had often wondered why, after her mother died, her father did not come home more often. He could have easily done so, seeing how short the journey was.

Then she remembered his explanation that he was continually required at Windsor Castle, which was in the other direction.

Linwood Priory had originally been the home of monks, who had inhabited the house for a hundred years before the Dissolution of the Monasteries.

Then it had reverted to the Church when Queen Elizabeth came to the throne, but it had become private at the end of her reign. She had honoured one of the early Linwoods, who had been of great support to her personally, by making a gift of The Priory to him.

And it became traditional in the family that they should always be in attendance at the Seat of Power and at the beck and call of the Monarch.

It was therefore not surprising that Queen Victoria was constantly seeking the advice of Lord Linwood.

He was very conscious of his own importance and with him duty always came first.

If his only daughter suffered because of his duty, he felt that she would understand, as if the Queen wanted him, he must at once be at Her Majesty's side.

Flavia had therefore felt when her mother died that she had lost not only one parent but two, and she had often wondered whether her mother had realised how much her father longed to be in London.

And how much he yearned to be in attendance at the Seat of Power.

But now, almost like a distant trumpet call, he had told Flavia to come to London.

Because her year of mourning was over there was no possible excuse for her not to obey him.

Everyone at The Priory, however, had felt ashamed, although they did not say so openly. It was wrong, they muttered over and over again among themselves, that Miss Flavia was so much alone.

Even if she still had to mourn for her mother, there should have been plenty of girls of her own age to keep her company.

Now, however, at the end of May, she had been freed.

Her father had duly sent for her to come to London exactly one day after her year of mourning was over.

'I suppose really,' she thought, 'I am feeling a little shy and nervous at going into the Social world after living so quietly in the country.'

After a moment another thought entered her head,

'Papa said I was to hurry. I wonder why.'

But as the carriage rumbled on, she knew it was no use discussing this with Martha.

The maid had closed her eyes and if she was not asleep, she obviously had no wish to talk and Flavia rather suspected that she felt sick in a carriage.

The horses were fresh and, as the roads were dry, they were moving at a fast rate towards London.

They stopped at a large coaching inn at luncheon time and Mr. Masters, Lord Linwood's private secretary in the country, had ordered a private room where Flavia could enjoy her luncheon.

She would much rather have eaten in the dining room with the other guests. It would have been interesting to see them and know who else was travelling as she was.

But it was no use her arguing against what was considered right and proper by her father.

She was well aware that because her maid was with her rather than a relative or a friend, it was correct that they should eat alone in a private room.

The luncheon was edible if rather dull and so they did not stay long.

As they set off again, Flavia told herself she must feel excited at nearing London and seeing her father and becoming a *debutante* that Season.

"Otherwise I will be too old, Papa," she had said when he talked to her about it.

"Don't be ridiculous," he had responded. "You are still only eighteen and, whilst some *debutantes* make their debut at seventeen, the correct age is eighteen."

Flavia did not argue that she would be nineteen the following month, as she had found, as others had found before her, that her father disliked being contradicted.

She supposed, when she was thinking it over, that as her father's daughter, she would be invited to a great number of parties.

It was rather frightening to think that she had in fact no personal friends she could look forward to meeting.

Her mother had not been very well for the last two years of her life and so they had entertained very little in the country. She had been very content just to be quietly with her husband and daughter.

When Flavia thought it all over, she came to the conclusion that she really had no close friends at all.

Except of course the horses and the dogs!

She had not been allowed to have a pet dog of her own and her father's dogs were kept in the stables, but she took them out with her whenever she went riding.

She thought that now her mother was dead, who had not been very fond of animals, she could persuade her father to allow her have two dogs in the house.

Yet, when he had come home for a short visit, there had been so many other pressing matters to discuss with him that she had not got round to asking.

They reached London just before four o'clock.

Martha had already said that she could do with a nice cup of tea and Flavia had told her it was certain to be waiting for them on their arrival.

There was one event that the servants never missed and that was teatime.

At The Priory Mrs. Ruck prided herself on her teas and there was always enough to eat in the drawing room for a great many more than just one slim girl.

As they turned into Grosvenor Square, Martha sat upright and pulled her hat down firmly over her forehead.

The horses came to a standstill outside one of the large houses overlooking the Square, and there was a pause before a footman opened the door of the carriage because the red carpet had to be run down over the pavement.

Flavia stepped out.

A smart butler she had not seen before, bowed.

"Welcome to London, Miss Flavia," he intoned. "His Lordship's expected back at six o'clock."

Flavia walked into the hall where there were four footmen in attendance and she saw, as she expected, there was a housekeeper in rustling black silk with a chatelaine at her waist at the top of the stairs.

"Mrs. Shepherd's waiting for you, miss," the butler said, "and tea'll be served in the downstairs sitting room."

"Thank you," Flavia managed to say. "I will come down as soon as I have taken off my hat and coat."

She remembered Mrs. Shepherd and shook her by the hand and the housekeeper then took her to one of the main bedrooms on the first floor.

It was an elegantly furnished room and, as Flavia looked around, she laughed and exclaimed,

"I'm glad I am now old enough to sleep here. I was rather afraid I might still be in the nursery!"

Mrs. Shepherd did not seem to think her remark particularly amusing and replied in a choked voice,

"Of course not, Miss Flavia. This is where you should be and his Lordship ordered that you were to be properly looked after. I've a lady's maid for you whose name is Bertha."

Flavia was glad when she saw Bertha that she was quite young and, according to Mrs. Shepherd, she had been well trained and was experienced.

They both assisted Flavia in taking off her hat and coat and poured hot water into the bowl on the washstand.

"Her Ladyship," Mrs. Shepherd said, "has ordered you a lot of clothes, Miss Flavia, and we've hung them in the wardrobe."

Flavia knew it was her Aunt Edith who had sent her the clothes she had been wearing in the country.

Although they were very attractive, she would have liked to choose for herself what she would wear in London.

However, when she looked at the clothes after Mrs. Shepherd had opened up the wardrobe, she was pleased to see that they were in the soft colours she liked and she felt sure they came from one of the best shops in Bond Street.

She remembered her father praising her aunt's good taste and he had also added,

"She only likes objects that are very expensive, as I found when she handed me the bill!"

Flavia sensed her father would not be particularly pleased at the large amount of clothes bought for her.

It was a matter she could hardly argue about. The clothes were there and she must wear them and what was clearly of little weight was her own opinion.

When she went downstairs for tea, she was to find that the sitting room was now quite different from how she remembered it. Her father must have rearranged all the furniture and the sofa and chairs were in different colours.

She had to admit it looked very nice, but even so there was something rather masculine and stiff about it.

She thought that her mother would have made it softer and in many ways more attractive.

'That is what I will have to do for Papa now,' she thought. 'But it will be difficult if he does not wish me to spend money on the house.'

She drank some tea and enjoyed the small delicious cakes and hot toast in a silver container.

Then she waited for her father.

When he came in, she ran to him and he kissed her affectionately.

"It is delightful to see you, Flavia," he said. "Now I have a busy programme for you, which I hope will make up for the long time you have had to spend in the country."

"It's so wonderful to be with you, Papa. You are looking well and I am sure having no more trouble with your back as you were at one time."

"Fortunately I have a doctor to take care of that and as I have been staying at Windsor Castle these past three or four weeks I have not had a bumpy journey to endure every time I went there. The rest has definitely done me good."

"Did you enjoy yourself, Papa?"

Lord Linwood smiled.

"One is always kept busy by Her Majesty and quite frankly, my dear, if one is in attendance one does not have time to think about oneself."

"I hope the Queen is going to spare you to me for a little while," said Flavia. "It will not be at all amusing to be in London, if I am not to be with you, Papa."

"You will see a great deal of me," he promised. "Also I have accepted many invitations for you, so that you will soon have little time to worry about me."

"I will always worry about you, Papa, because you are the one person I belong to."

Her father smiled.

"It is very sweet of you to say so, but I expect there will be many young men who will want you to spend your time with them. What is more, you will find them far more interesting than your father."

Flavia laughed.

"I will believe that only when it happens, Papa. At the same time, as I know no young men, I am very anxious to be with you."

"I promise you that we will be together as much as possible, my dear."

He sounded genuine, but she had the feeling that he was thinking of something quite different.

Flavia recognised that she might be wrong, but she had always been extremely perceptive where other people were concerned.

Her mother had often said to her,

"Tell me, my darling, what do you think about the person who has just called on us?"

Even when she was only twelve, Flavia had been able, her mother had told her later, to describe accurately the character of a stranger.

"How could you know," she said once, "that that woman who called on us last week was so extraordinary?"

The woman had turned out to be a fraud. She had wangled money from charities, which she had then put in her own pocket.

Flavia had listened to her and felt that the way she spoke was somehow insincere and the woman had in fact no real feelings for the poor people she professed to help. She had therefore saved her dear mother from contributing her money and her pity to no purpose.

She had also been helpful when they were engaging new servants or shopping where they were not known.

Her mother had always been interested in the shops that dealt in antiques, especially pictures that were sold as being painted by old Masters.

And it was quite remarkable the way Flavia would unerringly point out a fake being sold as a genuine article that had actually been made only a few years earlier and had dishonestly been aged artificially.

"How can you know these things, darling?" her mother had enquired. "I was completely deceived by that rather pretty ornament he offered us."

"He said it was very old, Mama, but I knew he was lying. I cannot tell you why. It just comes into my mind and funnily enough I always seem to be right."

"If you had lived a few hundred years earlier, you would have been burnt as a witch!" her father had joked.

Flavia had been only sixteen at the time and she had deliberately tried out her powers of recognising fraud or hypocrisy when she was sitting near people in Church or walking round at the local Flower Show.

When she was proved right, she was pleased that she possessed a gift her mother assured her was rare.

"At the same time, darling," she added, "you must be careful not to make a mistake. It would be terrible if you said that someone was fraudulent or wicked when they were really good. In fact you might seriously damage his or her life by what you said about them."

"I promise you, Mama, I will be very careful, but equally I have to say what I am told."

Her mother looked at her questioningly and then Flavia explained,

"It is just as if someone is telling me. They say something very softly in my ear and when I repeat it aloud, I find it's the truth."

Lady Linwood held up her hands.

"You frighten me, darling. It is undoubtedly a great gift, but you must be very careful with it."

"I will, Mama," Flavia had promised.

*

Now she was back in London, she could not help wondering if she would be able to separate the swans from the geese.

"Now tonight," her father was saying, "I have a very interesting man coming to dinner."

Before he could say any more, Flavia exclaimed,

"Oh, Papa, I had so hoped that you and I would be alone. It is something I have been looking forward to, so that I can tell you all about the new foals and all the news from the farms."

"We will have plenty of time for that, my dear. The man who has asked himself to dinner and who I may say is very keen to meet you is Lord Carlsby. He is in attendance on Her Majesty, as I am, and so seldom gets away from Windsor Castle that I could not refuse when he asked if he could dine with us tonight."

"I suppose not, Papa, but I am disappointed."

"I am sorry about that, but I am sure you will enjoy meeting him. He is very distinguished and I am delighted to be his friend."

When she was dressing for dinner, Flavia could not help feeling somewhat resentful.

Tonight at least she had wanted to be alone with her father.

He had handed her a list before they went upstairs and on it his secretary had written out all the balls, parties and luncheons he had already accepted on her behalf.

There were quite a number of them and when Lord Linwood gave it to her, he declared,

"I am sure this is just the beginning, my dear. By the end of this month you will be flooded with invitations, which will fill many pages rather than one or two in your engagement book."

"It is all very exciting, Papa, but I do want to see something of you. I have missed you very very much these last months and, whether it is in London or the country, I wish to be with you."

"And I want to be with you, my dear, but as you realise, I have to be at Her Majesty's call. That is why I have arranged for your aunt to take you to most of these parties."

Flavia had looked forward to being accompanied by her father and it had never struck her that he would provide her with just another chaperone.

For a brief moment she wanted to protest against this arrangement and then she knew it would do no good.

If her father was on call by the Queen, he had to obey her first.

His daughter certainly came second in line.

But Flavia could not help feeling that, if her mother had been alive, her father, however much he felt it was his duty, would have managed somehow to be with them both.

She was determined not to spoil her reunion with her father and if she protested, argued or tried to change what he had arranged, it would only annoy him.

She could not help but resent that Lord Carlsby was dining with them tonight as she could have had her father to herself if he had not pushed his way in.

When she had changed, she walked downstairs and found, although it was still a long time before dinner, that Lord Carlsby had already arrived.

As she entered the drawing room, the two men were talking earnestly to each other at the far end of the room.

However, they broke off immediately and rose to their feet as she walked towards them.

Flavia was in one of the pretty evening gowns her aunt had bought for her. It was certainly very becoming in the soft pink of the roses that grew so prolifically in the garden at The Priory.

She looked, although she was not aware of it, very lovely, as she moved across the room towards her father and the visitor.

She had no idea that they were both thinking that she might easily have stepped down from Mount Olympus or directly from Heaven.

"Oh, here you are, Flavia. I now want you to meet a good and kind friend of mine – Lord Carlsby."

Lord Carlsby held out his hand and remarked,

"You are even more beautiful than I expected, even though I knew that your father and mother *must* produce an exceptional daughter!"

Flavia smiled at him and he paid her several more compliments, but she did not feel particularly embarrassed.

Lord Carlsby was certainly an intelligent man and she listened attentively to the conversation at dinner and found it surprisingly interesting.

He and her father were discussing the situation in Europe and Her Majesty's handling of the difficulties they were encountering with the Russians.

"I can only be thankful," Lord Carlsby was saying, "that Mr. Disraeli is now Prime Minister. Her Majesty has such a dislike of Gladstone, I felt she might have a stroke!"

Lord Linford chuckled.

"You are quite right and we should be very grateful that Disraeli is there. He can always put her into a good temper."

"Even when he does fail occasionally," added Lord Carlsby, "then we all want to run for cover!"

Flavia smiled, as it was so unexpected to hear the Queen, of whom everyone was greatly in awe, being talked about in such an intimate manner.

As dinner progressed, she sensed that Lord Carlsby was looking her over in what she felt was a strange way.

He appeared to be appraising her, almost as if she was a horse for sale or a flower exhibited for a prize at a country show.

'I wonder why he should be so interested in me.' Flavia asked herself.

Then he was making her laugh at something he had said and again he was paying her extravagant compliments.

It was when dinner was over and they moved back into the drawing room that her father commented,

"I would hope, my dear, you will not think it rude, but Lord Carlsby and I have some very important matters to discuss which, being confidential, we cannot speak of in front of you."

"Are you telling me to go to bed, Papa?"

Flavia looked at the clock and the hands showed it was only half-past-nine.

"No, of course not. Just give us twenty minutes to talk these things over before Lord Carlsby has to leave us. Then you and I have a great deal to discuss."

Flavia smiled at him.

"Yes, indeed we have, Papa, and I will discreetly withdraw until you send for me."

She put down her coffee and walked to the door.

"Don't be too long," she urged, "or I will think you have forgotten about me."

"I promise not to," her father replied.

She went from the drawing room into the sitting room next door which her mother had turned into a library.

There was a large library in the house and a famous one at The Priory, but her mother had required books in London too as she was an avid reader.

She had therefore turned what was rather a dull and little used sitting room into an attractive library.

The books were all enclosed, not in cupboards but in shelves built onto the walls and there was not a bare wall in the whole room.

Amongst the books, some of which were centuries old, were, to Flavia's delight, several novels that had been published recently.

She decided that she would read them all and then wondered where she should start and looked towards the fireplace, which had a narrow bookcase on each side of it.

'I will start at the beginning,' Flavia told herself.

She opened the bookcase nearest to the fireplace to find several books that had been published in the last few years and which had not yet reached The Priory library.

She then pulled out two books by famous authors, deciding that she would take them up to her bedroom and start reading one before she went to sleep tonight.

As she pulled out another volume, to her surprise she could hear men's voices.

She suddenly became aware that it was her father's voice she was hearing and it was then she realised that the fireplaces in the two rooms must be back to back.

Thus there was one wall between the two rooms to which the bookshelves in this room had been attached.

She looked closely at the gap on the shelf left by the books she had removed and saw that there were some small holes in the wall behind them.

She could now hear quite clearly what her father was saying.

To her surprise he was talking about her.

"Do you really think, Carlsby" he was saying, "that Haugton will be attracted by Flavia? I have no wish for my daughter to be unhappy."

"Anyone who was married to Haugton would find him difficult," replied Lord Carlsby. "But he is without exception the best-looking young man in London. At the

17

same time, as you and I both know, her Majesty is seeing *far* too much of him."

"Do you think his advice to her is harmful?" asked Lord Linwood.

"I do think he is dangerous, simply because anyone who has influence over Her Majesty could interfere with our policy, especially in regard to – the Russians."

"We can always rely on Disraeli."

"Then we must thank Heaven for that," responded Lord Carlsby, "but he also, between ourselves, is finding Haugton a bit of a nuisance. Naturally he enjoys having, as he thinks, Her Majesty totally under his control."

"I think you are going too far when you say that, although I would agree that he is becoming a nuisance. I was most annoyed with him yesterday when the Queen put forward a new proposition that I knew had come directly from Haugton and which she had not thought of herself."

"We have to do something about him, Linwood, and personally I think my idea is an exceedingly good one, *especially* now that I have seen your daughter."

Lord Carlsby paused before he continued,

"Anyone who married her would be busy fending off a crowd of admirers and Haugton, as you well know, would not wish to take second place to someone who bore his name and was his wife."

"I agree with you and needless to say it would be an excellent marriage for my daughter. I suppose Haugton is one of the richest men in England and no one has a better ancestral home or a finer stable."

Lord Carlsby laughed.

"Horses! Horses! Always horses where you and your daughter are concerned. If nothing else proves easy in this marriage, they will both enjoy the finest and the fastest horses in the country."

There was silence for a moment.

Then very cautiously, Flavia pulled out yet another book so that she could hear even better.

She saw that the holes in the wall had been bored in a straight line and it looked as if they had been made at some time to support an object on the other side.

"I think it would be best," Lord Carlsby said rather slowly, as if he was thinking out every word, "to let your daughter meet Haugton quite normally at Social events."

"As you know, Haugton is coming to the dinner party I plan to give for Flavia the day after tomorrow and His Royal Highness, the Prince of Wales, will be present."

"I am sure that will be a useful start to our scheme," said Lord Carlsby. "If the Prince makes a fuss of Flavia, which he is bound to do, seeing how lovely she is, it will definitely make the Earl more interested in her."

He gave a sharp laugh before he went on,

"If nothing else, Haugton is a snob and he enjoys Royalty as other men have a preference for actresses and *cocottes*!"

"I suppose that's true, but Haugton is a big success wherever he goes. It is said that no woman can resist him."

"When he sees a pretty woman, he is irresistible," said Lord Carlsby. "That is why I think you will have no trouble in marrying your daughter to him."

"*No trouble*?" Lord Linwood repeated cynically. "I have heard that Haugton has said a thousand times that he has no intention of marrying, but will 'play the field'."

"I know that, but that is no reason why we should allow him to 'play our field' at Windsor and interfere with our guidance of the Queen."

"I agree with you, Carlsby. Equally I doubt if we can persuade him, however lovely my daughter may be, to offer her marriage."

"I think you are being rather stupid, if I may say so. You know, as I do, that there are a thousand unwritten laws as to what a man may do with a girl to ruin her reputation."

Lord Carlsby was becoming angry,

"You must have heard about what happened to poor Worcester – he only stood talking in the garden to that pretty creature he walked down the aisle with last week."

"What happened?" Lord Linwood asked.

"Her mother went straight to the Prince of Wales and told him her daughter's reputation was ruined. The Prince then told Worcester to 'behave like a gentleman' and he was therefore obliged to marry her."

"I heard the story, but thought it could not be true."

"Of course it's true," Lord Carlsby blustered, "and there should be no difficulty in your finding them alone in the garden or just staring at the stars without a chaperone."

There was a pause and then Lord Linwood said,

"I see your point. Very well, we will work on the way you suggest, meantime for Heaven's sake try to keep Haugton away from Windsor Castle."

"I will endeavour to do so, Linwood, but, if you ask my advice, the sooner he marries your daughter the more comfortable we can both be."

Lord Linwood gave a sigh.

"I suppose to be truthful, I am astonished that the Queen should be so infatuated with him."

"As I have said already, he is irresistible to every woman, but, like most men, he enjoys the Royal patronage and this can do much damage to our plans for Her Majesty.

"Unless the marriage to Flavia can take place as soon as possible, we can give up every hope of making Her Majesty listen sensibly to our suggestions as she did before Haugton burst in and upset the applecart."

"He has certainly done that. Very well, Carlsby, I agree with all you say and I will make sure that Flavia sits next to him at our dinner party the day after tomorrow."

"That is the first step in the right direction – "

"Now I will find Flavia," Lord Linwood said, rising to his feet. "Otherwise she will be suspicious as to why we sent her away."

"I see no reason for her to be suspicious, not at the moment at any rate."

"I am afraid my daughter may be difficult. I know it would be the most brilliant marriage she could possibly make. Haugton is so rich that even American millionaires look pale beside him."

"What more can you ask of a son-in-law?"

Lord Linwood did not answer.

Flavia knew that he was coming to look for her and swiftly she put the books back in the shelf.

She could hardly believe what she had just heard.

Yet now she knew what they were planning.

A moment later when her father opened the door, she was sitting demurely in a chair with another book open on her knee.

"It is over, my dear," he said. "We have had our talk and now Lord Carlsby wants you to come back. I am sure he will be leaving soon and then we can be alone."

Flavia managed to smile at him.

"That is what I have been waiting for, Papa," she said, "and I have a great deal to tell you."

CHAPTER TWO

After Lord Carlsby left, Flavia told her father all the news from The Priory.

He was extremely interested in the horses and in the crops that had been planted on the Home Farm and she also told him about the tenant farmers and how some of them had been encouraged to improve their productivity.

"We have more sheep and more chickens than we have ever had before," Flavia related.

"That is excellent, Flavia, and we must encourage them to expand and become more profitable every year."

"What they really need, Papa, is to see more of you. They are not going to listen to a woman and certainly not one as young as me. If you were there, I can see we would quickly become the most up-to date estate in the County."

Lord Linwood smiled.

"I appreciate your enthusiasm, my dear, but I am doing exceptionally difficult work at Court. As you know, Her Majesty relies on me in very many ways and I could not neglect her."

"Of course not, Papa, but then Her Majesty has the Prince of Wales to consult."

Lord Linwood was silent before replying,

"The Queen is totally convinced that the Prince is too flighty to be any help to her. I have, however, always believed it is essential for him to take some part in the ruling of our country."

"Of course it is. It would be just the same, Papa, as if you did not let me take an interest in every detail on our estate."

She had heard people gossiping that the Prince of Wales was only interested in enjoying himself and it was his mother who was determined he should not take any part in the political world she dominated.

Lord Linwood sighed.

He was aware, as was every man of intelligence at Court, that the Prince was being deliberately shut out.

Granted the Queen had been shocked at the way he enjoyed the high life of London and Paris and at his friends who encouraged him to be, in her mind, a roué.

But the older courtiers like Lord Linwood and Lord Carlsby knew that his rakish behaviour with actresses and *courtesans* had a different aspect.

Previously they had dismissed it as the excesses of youth, but now that had changed.

It had become a way of life, a compensation for the frustrations caused by his mother and thus an outlet for his energy.

The Prince was rich, he was married, he was the father of six children and he enjoyed enormous prestige.

He was heir to the throne of Great Britain.

Just as in his adolescence, it was the story of a boy denied all that made life exciting and in the prime of life he was still deprived of the Royal power that he should have been trained to handle.

This had evoked a gathering frustration, but he was so very keen on his perceived duties that no Royal had ever opened more Public Libraries, laid more Foundation stones or attended more Official Ceremonies.

It was said that a whole room had been put aside at Marlborough House to store his various uniforms and two valets were engaged to brush and care for them.

Yet all the Prince had, as Lord Linwood knew, was just a minute portion of the real power he craved.

Even among his friendships the Prince was actively seeking power, and it had passed through Lord Linwood's mind some time ago that the Prince of Wales might in some way be used to prevent the Earl of Haugton being so welcome at Windsor Castle.

When he had planned the dinner party he intended to give in two days' time, he was thinking that perhaps the Prince of Wales would be helpful in disposing of the Earl in several different ways.

As Flavia stopped talking about The Priory, he said,

"Now then, my dear, I have a surprise for you that I know you will appreciate."

"What is it, Papa?" she enquired nervously.

"I know that you will be inundated with invitations from your mother's friends and mine. But, in order to set you off on exactly the right foot, I have arranged a party for the day after tomorrow that I know you will find totally different from any party you have ever been to before."

"What is happening, Papa?" Flavia asked him even more nervously.

"I have invited His Royal Highness, the Prince of Wales to dinner here – and he has accepted."

Flavia stared at him.

"His Royal Highness! But Papa *how* exciting! I never thought I would ever meet him."

"You will be the hostess the day after tomorrow for dinner, and I have also asked the Earl of Haugton, who is one of the smartest and most interesting young gentlemen in Society."

Flavia drew in her breath sharply.

She had only just leant why the Earl of Haugton had been invited.

"Lord Carlsby is coming too, also a great number of amusing and beautiful ladies and naturally for you, my dear, some charming young gentlemen. Although I doubt if any of them will be as handsome and certainly not as rich as the Earl of Haugton."

"It sounds absolutely fascinating, Papa, and I will be thrilled to meet the Prince of Wales."

"What I want you to do, Flavia, is to make quite certain that your aunt has chosen a really fantastic gown for you to wear that evening, and for you to look through your mother's jewellery."

Flavia stared at him in surprise, but he went on,

"It has been kept in the safe here. Choose what will enhance your appearance without being too overdressed for a *debutante*."

"You are very kind, Papa, and it will be wonderful to have such a party in our own house."

"I would like actually," her father added, "to have given you a little breathing-space before you made your dramatic appearance into the great Social world, but I had to choose a day when the Prince of Wales could be present and he has chosen the day after tomorrow. As he has so many other appointments, I could not argue with him."

"No, of course not, Papa," agreed Flavia.

Equally, as she thought it all over when she went upstairs to bed, it all seemed very strange.

Why had her father asked her to meet the Earl of Haugton, whom he and Lord Carlsby wanted her to marry, at the same time as the Prince of Wales?

She had, of course, no idea that once again the two courtiers were trying to use their power not only with the Queen but also with the Prince of Wales.

It was true that in her middle fifties Queen Victoria showed no sign of giving up or allowing her son even a particle of power.

Yet it was always wise to anticipate the future and clearly Lord Linwood and Lord Carlsby were determined to keep their positions at Court whoever sat on the throne.

The two elderly men had planned the dinner party together and it included the Prince's closest friends such as the Duke of Sutherland, Lord Aylesford, Lord Carrington and Lord Charles Beresford.

If they accepted, the Prince would accept too.

Lord Linwood was certain that His Royal Highness would be very captivated by the beauty of Flavia as well as interested and amused by the Earl of Haugton, who, being younger than the Prince and his close associates, had up to now hardly met him.

He had not yet been invited to Marlborough House and both Lord Linwood and Lord Carlsby were sure that, if the Prince of Wales now became interested in the Earl, his influence at Windsor Castle would fade.

What was more, the Prince could always be relied on to assist and push a love affair and would undoubtedly, as he had done on several other occasions, help anguished parents who believed their daughter had lost her reputation.

In fact Lord Linwood thought he and Lord Carlsby had been exceedingly clever in arranging the dinner party.

It seemed impossible for it to be a failure and what, however, made the party even more significant was that unexpectedly the Prince of Wales had lost his heart.

The lady was extremely beautiful, unusual, and was already known as the 'Jersey Lily'.

Mrs. Langtry had come to London from Jersey with a meek weak husband and no money.

She was so lovely that everyone who met her talked about her endlessly and acclaimed her as a great beauty.

It was arranged that the Prince of Wales should meet her after the Opera and it was really not surprising that within a month Mrs. Langtry became the Prince's first mistress to be openly recognised by the Social world.

As he was so infatuated with her, no invitation was extended to the Prince unless Mrs. Langtry was invited too.

If Lord Linwood had not been persona grata with the Queen at Windsor Castle, the Prince would doubtless not have dreamt of accepting an invitation to dinner at Linwood House.

But he too had an axe to grind.

Although so far Lord Linwood and Lord Carlsby had failed to persuade his mother to let him partake in the Government even in the smallest way, he always went on hoping.

He was therefore prepared to honour them with his presence, provided that Mrs. Langtry was invited too.

Flavia was amazed at the importance of the guests at the party her father was giving for her and for the first time she had some idea of how powerful he was at Court.

And how obsessive he and Lord Carlsby were that no one should ever interfere with their influence over the Queen.

Her father was describing the guests and giving her a short biography of each one and she began to realise how very dangerous he and Lord Carlsby considered this Earl of Haugton to be – and how determined they were to move him from Windsor Castle to Marlborough House.

Flavia had been in the country where she had no one to talk to but the horses, but she had read not just the books in the library but the daily newspapers.

Her father had made it a habit when he was a young man to take every daily and weekend newspaper published and so Flavia had learnt a great deal about political affairs.

She was thus far more knowledgeable about politics than many men twice or three times her age.

She followed with interest the revolt in the Turkish province of Herzegovina in the summer of 1875 and a year later Serbia declared war on Turkey and then thousands of Russian volunteers poured into Belgrade.

The next year war stories began to appear in the British papers and it was reported that twelve thousand victims were alleged to have been slaughtered by the Turks in Bulgaria.

Mr. Gladstone, the Leader of the Opposition, made furious speeches against the unspeakable Turks and yet no one Flavia knew seemed at all perturbed.

Her father, however, told her that the Queen was horrified.

A Russian Army, although poorly organised and under corrupt leadership, was marching on Constantinople and was within sixty miles of its walls.

Flavia had read of the Queen's anger and was quite sure that it was on her father's suggestion that six ironclads stationed in Besika Bay were sent through the Dardanelles.

After some delay the ships steamed to the Island of Prinkipo in the Sea of Marmora and dropped anchor within sight of Constantinople and it was that, Flavia was to learn later, which alarmed the Grand Duke Nicholas, who was in charge of the Russian Army.

He was then forced to turn back and because she was living in the country, she had not heard people singing in London,

"We don't want to fight
But by jingo if we do
We've got the ships, we've got the men
We've got the money too."

She asked everyone she knew to tell her what was happening, but they knew very little and so Flavia had to wait until her father came home for a short visit to learn that the Russians had admitted,

"We have sacrificed one hundred thousand picked soldiers and ten millions of money for nothing."

Now she began to see that her father wanted no opposition to himself and Lord Carlsby at Windsor Castle and they needed to nip any likely challenger in the bud.

When Flavia retired to her bedroom that night, she read through the list of people who had been invited to what was called 'her' dinner party.

She was now well aware that it was just a clever way of removing the Earl of Haugton from Windsor Castle and preventing him from taking Lord Linwood's and Lord Carlsby's place beside the Queen.

'It's still 'wheels within wheels',' she thought, 'and I am just a pawn in their hands.'

She could easily understand, having overheard the secret conversation between the two older men what they were up to.

If the Earl of Haugton would become a friend and a confidant of the Prince of Wales, the Queen would no longer believe in him.

Better still, if he was married and far away on his honeymoon, he would not be in a position to continue his nefarious influence on Her Majesty.

It was a clever and well thought out plan.

Flavia's father had told her,

"It's just a small private party, but I have engaged a band to play in the ballroom and there will be card tables for those who prefer gambling to dancing."

"But Papa, how many people do you expect?" she had enquired.

"I think we will be thirty for dinner and perhaps the same number will come in when dinner is over."

Flavia was silent – and for the moment, she was too astonished to think clearly.

Her father had always intended to give her a ball and luncheon parties so that she could make new friends.

She recognised now, however, that he must be very anxious with regard to his own position at Windsor Castle to have arranged it all so hastily.

She had expected to take everything slowly – to go to only a few parties to start with, then gradually increase them to include everything by the end of the Season.

Now, she was actually starting with the Prince of Wales coming to Linwood House to dine, accompanied by the beautiful Mrs. Langtry.

She was slipping into the Social world from the top.

It was exciting – it was thrilling.

But at the same time Flavia was desperately afraid.

Her father might succeed in marrying her off to the Earl of Haugton almost before she had even had a glimpse of the *Beau Monde*.

It was just by chance and a very lucky one, that she had overheard the two courtiers' plan.

She had no intention, whatever they might say, of marrying a man she did not love and who did not love her.

She was only too well aware that she was crossing a very dangerous bridge.

One slip and she would be submerged in the water beneath, which was, of course, marriage to the man they were planning to marry her off to.

Now she thought about it, she remembered she had read his name quite often in the Social columns amongst those who had been present at some function or who were guests at a ball or a concert.

Her father seemed to have convinced himself that she would most conveniently fall in love with the Earl of Haugton, but she could only feel that he was behaving in a strange and unfeeling way towards her.

She was quite certain that she would find it difficult to prevent him achieving all he had set out to do.

She looked back to the days when she had heard her aunts and her father's friends talking about Social life in London. She had not been that interested except when they talked about the racing at Ascot or the parties that had taken place at Marlborough House.

Now that she was part of it, she realised it was all of great significance and there were endless manoeuvrings behind every event – and behind every thought and word.

How could she have imagined for a single moment that her father and Lord Carlsby would use her to be rid of a young man who was being a nuisance to them at Windsor Castle?

A man they felt was undermining their authority with the Queen.

But that was not a matter she should be involved in.

She also realised that while they wished to capture the Earl for her, they believed that he would be delighted to be invited to a party attended by the Prince of Wales.

Looking back, Flavia could recall her father talking to her mother about Lord Carlsby, telling her how vital it was that he should be at Windsor Castle to support him in his advice to the Queen on both home and foreign affairs.

This had been nearly ten years ago when Benjamin Disraeli had become Prime Minister for the first time, but had been forced to resign after only a few months and Mr. Gladstone had taken his place.

Flavia fully realised that the Queen did not like Mr. Gladstone and was continually fighting with him over the country's foreign policy.

Lords Linwood and Carlsby had then clung even more desperately to their position as her advisers.

Flavia had heard her father say that on one occasion when Russia's policy became aggressive, Queen Victoria had become hysterical and had even threatened to abdicate.

"If England is about to kiss Russia's feet," she had written to Disraeli, now again Prime minister, who had shown her letter to Lord Linwood, *"the Queen will not be a party to the humiliation of England and will lay down the Crown."*

In another letter Her Majesty had said,

"Oh! If the Queen were only a man, she would give those horrid Russians, whose word one cannot trust, such a beating!"

Flavia had been interested and yet she did not ask her father many questions because her mother said it bored him, as he had quite enough questions to answer when he was on duty and at home he wanted to relax.

Now when it all flooded back into Flavia's mind, she could understand her father's feelings.

Just how could he possibly allow this young Earl, because he was so good-looking, to influence the Queen on matters he considered of great national importance.

'At the same time,' she told herself firmly, 'I have no intention of marrying this Earl of Haugton. If they cannot be rid of him except by using me as a pawn in their hands, they will just have to put up with him!'

The whole situation was so unexpected for Flavia and so horrifying that it was impossible for her to sleep.

*

Flavia climbed out of bed and walked across to the window to draw back the curtains.

In the country she would have looked out onto the garden with the moonlight turning everything to silver – it made the huge fountain in the centre of the lawn seem to be throwing hearts of gold up towards the sky.

Now she was looking out on Grosvenor Square.

The trees seemed insignificant and the statue too was unimpressive.

Nevertheless this was London.

This was where things really happened and she was willy-nilly part of them.

'I have to be clever, very clever,' she told herself, 'but at least Papa does not know that I am aware of his intention. Equally it is very frightening and something I could never have expected when I left home.'

For a moment she felt an urge to run away.

To be back in the quietness and the peace of The Priory and to ride alone over the fields and into the woods inhabited by the goblins and fairies of her imagination.

Then she told herself she must not be a coward.

For the first time in her life, she was now up against something bigger than anything she had ever faced before.

'I will not let it defeat me,' she vowed. 'I feel sure Mama will help me, but I have to use my brain and, more important still, my instinct to know what is right and what is wrong.'

Because she felt the view outside the window was no help to her, she pulled back the curtain and got into bed.

As she lay back on her pillows, she had the feeling that she had suddenly grown up.

From being in many ways just a child she was now mentally older, stronger and more determined than she had been – reaching not for earthly possessions of which she was fortunate to have so many, but for something that was indefinable and spiritual.

It was this that would help her in what she knew was going to be a battle. A battle with the one member of her family who really mattered – her father.

She had known, ever since she was a child, that he was a very determined man. He invariably had his way not only with her mother, who adored him, but with everyone in his life.

'Yet in this instance,' she told herself, 'he is going to be the loser and not the winner!'

If she was now to fight him as effectively as he was planning to organise her and her future, she would need *his* intelligence and *his* strength to defeat him.

'I can do it! I know I can do it!' Flavia told herself, 'and I will have to be even more astute than Papa and use my gift of perception as it has never been used before.'

She drew in her breath.

Then, almost instinctively, she prayed softly,

'*Please God help me.*'

*

The next morning Flavia woke up before the maid came to call her and she realised she had slept peacefully all through the night.

She had imagined she would lie awake worrying over what would happen to her, but, as if her prayers had soothed away her doubts and fears, she felt at peace. Not only with herself but with the world outside.

When she went down to breakfast, it was to find that her father was already eating.

He was in a hurry to go to Number 10 Downing Street as he had an appointment with the Prime Minister.

"I do hope, Papa, to meet Mr. Disraeli while I am in London," said Flavia. "I have read so much about him and admire him enormously."

"You are quite right, my dear. He is a great man. The Queen does like being with him and encourages him to spend as much time as possible at Windsor Castle."

"Is there anything you particularly want me to do, Papa? And will you be back for luncheon?"

"We will have luncheon together and if I am free, I will take you to call on one or two friends who I know will be useful to you."

"That will be wonderful, Papa."

"And don't forget I want you to look through your mother's jewellery for tomorrow night. I have also given my secretary the names of others who should be asked to come in after dinner. I suggest you look at the list so that you know who they are when they arrive."

"Of course I will, Papa. I am looking forward to the party, especially to meeting His Royal Highness."

"I want you also to take notice of the young man I mentioned before, the Earl of Haugton, my dear. He is most intelligent, has a huge fortune and is pursued by every ambitious mother in the whole of London."

"You mean he is unmarried?" she asked innocently.

"Of course he is unmarried, but he is twenty-eight and sooner or later he will have to marry to produce an heir.

I believe that his relatives are already pleading with him to do so."

"I hope he has the strength to refuse them," Flavia remarked. "One should marry only because one is in love and not because one wants a son or, as the case may be, a title."

Her father smiled.

"You will learn it is really most important. It has always been a deep regret to me that I did not have a son, not only to carry on the title but to live in The Priory and feel as we do that he is part of it."

"Which, of course, we are, Papa. It has been there for hundreds of years and I am certain that whoever takes over from you will treat it with respect and love."

Her father did not answer.

She knew, as she had indeed known all her life, that he fervently wished that she was a boy rather than a girl.

Because she did not want him to think about that at this moment, Flavia asked him,

"Will you be seeing Lord Carlsby today?"

"I doubt it. He will be at Windsor Castle. It is so essential that he should be with Her Majesty and keep out others who are undesirable."

He spoke the words almost violently and Flavia smiled to herself.

It seemed ridiculous that this Earl of Haugton could topple two such eminent gentlemen from their beloved position of power.

Her father rose from the table.

"I will be back at twelve o'clock," he said, "and I will take you to luncheon with one of my friends. Then I hope we will call on some more this afternoon. Look your prettiest and remember, if the Dowagers disapprove of you, you are quickly, in some peculiar way, dropped Socially."

Flavia laughed.

"You are not frightening me, Papa. You know that everyone will be pleased to accept me as your daughter. I promise you I will behave exactly as Mama would want me to."

"I know that," her father replied. "The trouble is we have too many people nowadays barging into places where they should keep out – and making trouble."

Again he was bitter and Flavia was convinced that the Earl of Haugton had really got under her father's skin and Lord Carlsby's.

'It's almost like a game,' she thought 'except that they take it so seriously.'

She wondered if the Earl of Haugton knew how apprehensive he had made them.

Once her father had left, she went into the library.

She took out the books she had removed yesterday just to make sure she had not been dreaming when she had overheard the conversation between the two courtiers.

The small holes were still there.

She replaced the books in case anyone else should realise, as she had, that it was a listening-post.

'It just shows,' she mused, 'how careful one should be. One day I must warn Papa in case anyone who is his enemy listens to him and does him untold harm.'

She chose some more books from the other side of the library to take upstairs to her bedroom.

She then dressed for her father to introduce her into the Social world.

She could not help feeling that if it had been a year ago, before her mother had died, she would have felt very differently from the way she felt now.

She was not really certain what she did feel.

Only that she was older, wiser and certainly more determined than she had ever been before.

She would not be manoeuvred, pushed or forced into doing anything she did not wish to do.

Especially when it concerned marriage.

Her father and mother had been so happy together. He had never looked at anyone else, nor had she.

Yet, although Flavia could not exactly put it into words, she knew that she wanted more.

She wanted something other people seldom had but which everyone sought.

It was the love she had read about in books.

Love that men had fought for, died for and even been crucified for.

It was the great love that was not only physical but spiritual.

And which had caused revolutions and misery since the world began.

But it had also given people a desire for what every man in his heart believed he was entitled to.

'I suppose in a way,' Flavia reflected, 'that is why I have educated myself so that I can help any man I love whatever he is doing. Also so that I can love someone who is himself everything I am seeking.'

She realised only too well that *debutantes* and all young girls wanted to marry a man with money and who was of standing in the Social world.

Flavia had always thought that was a stupid way of looking at life.

After all, even if the man you married was a Duke and you then became a grand Duchess, it would be small compensation to be bowed to and asked to open Flower Shows if your husband was not interested in you.

'What I want,' Flavia had said to herself when she was quite young, 'is a man who will love me because I am *me* and not because my father is a Lord or my mother is a great beauty. I must be the most important person in the world in his eyes, just as he must be in mine.'

She had often thought about this riding alone in the woods.

She had often wondered when she saw a bride and groom coming out of the village Church how much they meant to each other.

Was the world really wonderful for them because they were in love?

She knew perceptively that most of their friends who came to The Priory to see her father and mother were not really happy.

They might be influential, they might be rich, they might boast a title, yet she knew that there was something missing in their lives.

She could feel that they had little to look forward to and that they were not living their precious lives to the full.

When she studied them with her strange power of perception, she recognised that something was missing.

None of them looked forward to a wonderful and exciting life ahead.

'There is something wrong,' she told herself, 'and it is something I definitely don't want.'

She had thought it all out most carefully this last year before coming to London.

Of course she realised that all *debutantes*, and she was no exception, wanted to be married.

They longed to meet the perfect man who would love them. A man who would give them a life of sunshine and happiness with children to ensure that their marriage was complete.

And Flavia was sensible enough to realise that this happened very rarely and if she wanted it to happen to her, she would have to be very careful.

The man who said that he loved her must not be impressed by her father's power and influence.

Nor by his title.

Nor by The Priory and its large estate.

Nor by the money she herself would inherit when her father died.

All these thoughts dazzled like stars around her.

What she desired was a man who would love and adore her, even if she had been born in the gutter with nothing to offer him but her heart and her soul.

'I suppose,' Flavia mused as she walked down the stairs, 'I am asking the impossible. Papa has asked his friends to be kind to his motherless daughter and they will not fail him. And yet secretly he and Lord Carlsby have already decided what to do with me. *That* I will never tolerate nor will I ever agree to it!'

As she reached the bottom of the stairs, she gave a little laugh.

'As it happens,' she determined, 'I dislike the Earl already, just because he threatens like a dark cloud to spoil my introduction to the *Beau Monde*.'

CHAPTER THREE

Flavia had an enjoyable luncheon with her father's friends and one of her distant cousins.

They were interested to hear about The Priory and Flavia sensed that they were longing to be asked to stay.

They were also curious as to which parties she had been invited to.

She noticed her father was careful not to say that His Royal Highness was coming to dinner and so she too stayed quiet about it, but she was sure that they would not only feel envious but would then turn up somehow to meet the Prince!

After they had left, her father remarked,

"You were very tactful, my dear. I realised at once that I had not told you to keep your lips sealed about our Royal visitor tomorrow night."

"I knew you had not asked them and they would be disappointed if I mentioned it, Papa."

"You are a very bright girl, my dear, and you would make an excellent wife for a diplomat."

Flavia realised that her father was speaking without thinking and she therefore quickly responded,

"I think that is a really fascinating idea, because I could travel with him and see the world."

Her father became silent and she knew he thought he had been rather tactless and it would be a mistake to go further with the subject.

She was about to ask him to tell her more about life at Windsor Castle and instead he looked anxiously at his watch before saying,

"You must forgive me, my dear, if I leave you with your aunt who has been so kind in buying your clothes. I have an urgent appointment at three with the Secretary of State for Foreign Affairs and I must not be late."

"Of course not, Papa, when will you be home?"

He hesitated.

"I hope to be back by six o'clock and we will have an early dinner. We are bound to be late tomorrow night."

"I am so looking forward to my party, Papa."

"You deserve it, my dear. You have been so good and uncomplaining about being alone in the country. I am sure most girls would have been writing me letters begging to be brought to London."

"You were quite right to wait until I was out of mourning, Papa. Nothing would be more depressing than trying to look pretty and be amusing when wearing black."

"Well, now you are free to wear any colour you want. You will look lovely in every one of them."

"That is a very nice compliment, Papa. I hope for your sake I will receive a great many more."

He dropped her at a large house in Belgrave Square where her aunt and some friends were expecting her.

She was disappointed when he only came into the drawing room, kissed his sister-in-law and declared,

"I am going to be late for my appointment, and you know what a stickler the Marquis of Salisbury can be for punctuality. So forgive me, Edith, and look after Flavia. I will send a carriage for her after tea."

With that he had gone.

Flavia, feeling somewhat apologetic, faced her aunt and her friends. And most fortunately her Aunt Edith, the Viscountess Midstock, was a very effusive person.

She kissed Flavia affectionately, introduced her to everyone present, making amusing remarks about each of them as she did so.

Everyone was laughing by the time Flavia had met them all and then her aunt said,

"I knew you were coming this afternoon and I have bought more clothes for you. I saw yesterday some very pretty gowns and I could not resist them. One is for the smartest party you will attend first."

It was with difficulty that Flavia prevented herself from saying that would be tomorrow night, so she replied,

"How exciting, Aunt Edith! I am thrilled with all the clothes you have already found for me."

Everyone remarked that what she was wearing was delightful and it was some time before her aunt could take her upstairs to see the gowns she had purchased.

The moment she saw the best one, Flavia knew it was the prettiest gown she had ever imagined, let alone had the chance of wearing.

It was of course white, but the frills and the flowers that ornamented it were all edged with endless diamante, which would glitter every time she moved.

She only just prevented herself from saying that she would wear her mother's jewellery tomorrow night and a diamond necklace would go perfectly with the gown.

"Thank you, thank you," she enthused to her aunt. "You have been so kind to me and I now have a complete trousseau."

Aunt Edith turned and looked at Flavia.

"That is what I am afraid of, dear child. Anyone as pretty as you is easily rushed into marriage. Not only do they not know their husband well, but they don't know the sort of life they will be leading – it is often very different from the one they have been born into."

She paused and Flavia parried with a smile,

"What you are really saying, Aunt Edith, is that I am not to be in a hurry."

"Exactly. As you are so pretty, you will doubtless have a dozen men wanting you to be their wife, but don't jump at the first or for that matter the second or the third. Get to know him well and make quite certain you want to spend the rest of your life with him."

Flavia thought that this was very good advice and what she herself actually meant to do.

She kissed her aunt and sighed,

"I am very very grateful for all the beautiful clothes you have bought for me."

She smiled before she added,

"I promise you, Aunt Edith, I will take your advice and think very carefully before I marry anyone."

"I know that you are going to be a great success, Flavia."

They talked together for some time and then in case it seemed rude to her aunt's friends, they went down to the drawing room.

Everyone was talking about the parties they had already enjoyed and the ones that would take place in the next two months.

"I am sure your aunt has made sure you are invited by everyone who is of any significance," one of the ladies said. "But if at any time you feel lonely in that big house and your father is very busy, do come to me and be with my daughter and sons. They will find something amusing for you to do."

Flavia laughed, but thought her offer was very kind and friendly.

By the time the carriage came for her, she thought she had already made some friends in London whom she would very much like to see again.

She had been surprised that her father had not asked her aunt to the party tomorrow night, but she understood why when her aunt insisted on driving back to Grosvenor Square with her.

"There is one young man," she began, "I must warn you about in case you meet him and, like most of the girls who are 'coming out' this year, you fall in love with him."

"Who can that be?" Flavia enquired.

"I don't suppose that you would have heard of him down in the country, but he is the Earl of Haugton. He is, I suppose, the most popular young gentleman of this Season or any other Season for that matter."

She spoke rather scathingly and Flavia quizzed her,

"Do tell me about him, Aunt Edith."

"He is very good-looking. In fact women, to my mind, make fools of themselves because they think he is so handsome. But he is of Social consequence because he is an Earl and extraordinarily rich."

"Do the girls really fall in love with him?"

"Unfortunately yes, not only the young girls, but, of course, you should know nothing about that sort of gossip. What I am really saying in simple language is you are *not* to fall in love with him."

"I think that most unlikely – but why not?"

She saw her aunt was hesitating for the right words and then she continued,

"He is used to women almost swooning because he is so handsome, so he is, not unnaturally, conceited. At the same time he pays little attention to *debutantes*. Whenever I have observed him at a ball, he is dancing with married women, who look up at him with an expression that should infuriate their husbands!"

Flavia laughed because she could not help it.

"You make the Earl sound very extraordinary, Aunt Edith."

"I suppose in a way he is extraordinary," her aunt admitted grudgingly. "Equally I don't want you to waste your time running after a man, as the other girls are doing, who has no intention of marrying. In fact, he told me so himself."

"What did you say to him, Aunt Edith?"

"I told him he was very wise, but one day he would fall in love and then everything would be different."

"Did he believe you?"

"No, of course not. He is quite content with people fawning over him and making a fuss of him. In fact some of the women behave in a manner that shocks me."

"Then he must be very very good-looking?"

"He is, and, as I said, he is also very rich and has a distinguished title. I can easily understand the silly little *debutantes* thinking that he will propose to them and they will queen it in his magnificent houses."

Aunt Edith hesitated and then carried on,

"If you get the chance, by all means go to Haugton House in Park Lane to look at the furniture, the pictures, the china and the library, but *not* at the owner!"

Flavia laughed.

"You make it sound so funny, Aunt Edith, that now I am quite curious about this man."

"Of course you are. That is why I am warning you that he will pay very little attention to you."

"Why should he, Aunt Edith?"

"He is much too clever to be caught by ambitious mothers and too sensible to think that a young girl would keep him happy as his wife."

"Well, I promise to be careful not to lose my heart."

"Perhaps I have been wrong in making you curious about him, but he is a danger. I have had two girls crying on my shoulder, saying how much they loved him. They thought because he had paid them a polite compliment or two that he loved them. These silly creatures soon learnt better, but I have no wish to see you crying for Vincent Haugton."

"I promise you I will not do that. Forewarned is forearmed and you are quite right, as I am from the country and very ignorant about London, to warn me of any such dangers."

"There are plenty of them, Flavia. So don't forget, my dearest, that since your father is a rich man and you are his only child, you will undoubtedly have a large dowry when you marry."

She saw Flavia looked surprised and added,

"What I am warning you about now is the fortune-hunters. They always appear at this time of year and there were two marriages I attended recently and knew that, even before the ring was on the bride's finger, that the marriage would be a disaster."

"You mean the man married her for her money?"

"That is putting it bluntly and accurately. I often feel depressed when I think of those poor girls who give their hearts to men who are completely unworthy of them."

"You did not warn them?" enquired Flavia.

Aunt Edith shook her head.

"There is nothing more stupid or blind than a girl in love. She sees a man not as he is, but as she wants him to be. The disillusionment comes later when they are married and then there is *no* escape."

Her aunt spoke so solemnly that Flavia wanted to laugh, but she felt it would be rude.

She knew her aunt was very fond of her, because she had loved her mother so much and she was therefore trying to mother her.

Flavia fully realised that she was genuinely worried about her and, almost as if she was reading her thoughts, Aunt Edith remarked,

"You might think I am making a fuss, dear child, but I assure you I am speaking because I want you to be as happy as your father and mother were and as I was with my beloved husband until he died."

"Of course I want that. You are quite right to warn me where I might make mistakes. As you must be aware, since Mama died I have lived alone almost all the time at The Priory. Papa is always in London or Windsor Castle and few local people bothered about me. So I only had the horses and the dogs to talk to."

"I ought to have come and stayed with you more often, but I too had many obligations in London and it was difficult to get away."

"I am not reproaching you, Aunt Edith. I am only grateful for all you are telling me now."

"My advice is quite simple, Flavia. Enjoy yourself, but don't take any man too seriously, not until you know him well. Hesitate a dozen times before you say 'yes'."

"I will promise you, Aunt Edith, but you seem sure I will have a great number of proposals. I am not greedy and will be quite content with just one or two!"

"I don't mind predicting that you will have a great many more. I just want you to be careful of the men who try to sweep you off your feet and up the aisle before you have really considered what sort of life you will lead once the honeymoon is over."

"I have already promised you I will not do anything in haste, Aunt Edith, and I am so grateful for the warning, especially about the Earl of Haugton."

"It's ridiculous the way women run after him and I think they make complete fools of themselves and some of them should be old enough to know better!"

"It must be great fun for him," remarked Flavia.

"Unfortunately," her aunt said sharply, "the Earl of Haugton has *everything*, but everything he could possibly need. I am told that the Queen herself is devoted to him."

Flavia knew this already and she also thought, after all she had just heard about the Earl of Haugton, he would undoubtedly be a disappointment when she did meet him.

And that would frustrate her Papa.

Her father was afraid of him and dozens of women were apparently in love with him!

He sounded like the hero in a cheap novel or one of the Gods from Olympus and not much in between!

The whole situation was ridiculous.

Equally she realised that he was a danger, although not in the way her aunt meant.

Both her father and Lord Carlsby were planning to ensnare him – and she was to be the sacrificial victim.

'I have to be astute about this,' she told herself.

When the carriage returned to Grosvenor Square, Aunt Edith came in for a moment.

"This house has never been the same since your dear mother died, Flavia, but I have always thought it one of the most attractive and charming houses in London."

"That is what I hope to make it for Papa," Flavia replied, "as long as I am here with him."

"Quite right, my dearest, and do persuade him to be with you and not spend so much time at Windsor Castle."

"That is exactly what I want too, Aunt Edith, but it will not be easy."

"I can understand, your father enjoys his influence, which I assure you is very real. I have always heard that the Queen is not only fond of him but relies on him to help and guide her in the present difficult situation."

"You mean as regards the Russians," said Flavia.

Her aunt nodded.

"I think the real danger is now over, but there are others and while the Empire grows bigger and bigger, more and more problems arise. So you will have to look after your father and not let him do too much."

Flavia spread out her hands.

"The difficulty has always been to persuade Papa to do anything he does not want to do. Even Mama found that."

"I know, my dear, but you are the one person who can convince him not to over-exert himself or to care too much about the goings-on at Windsor Castle. It makes him neglect his home and those of us who love him."

She spoke sincerely and Flavia sensed that she was really worried about him and thought that her aunt would worry much more if she knew what he was planning, and how she was to be sacrificed so that the most handsome man in London should lose his influence over the Queen.

'The whole thing is ridiculous' she thought again and then she said aloud,

"I will try to remember everything you have told me, Aunt Edith. And I would be so grateful if you would warn me from time to time not only about Papa, but about anyone I meet who may not be completely desirable."

"Of course I will, dear child. What I have been saying to you is simply not to lose your head too quickly, and especially *not* to the Earl of Haugton."

"I will get it firmly in my mind," promised Flavia.

Her aunt kissed her and then she drove away.

*

Alone, Flavia started to explore the house to see if there were many alterations.

There was a new piano, which was more up-to-date than the one they had had before and there were two new pictures she had not seen.

Otherwise, except for the sitting room, things had not been moved or altered since she was last here.

She looked at the time and thought that her father would not be coming back just yet and she knew that there would be tea waiting for him in the study.

It was a room she had always sat in with her father when they were alone.

His writing desk was still there and on it she could see a table plan that had been worked out by his secretary for dinner tomorrow night and she reckoned that most of the guests who had been invited had already accepted.

When she looked for her own name, she felt that she would find it beside the Earl of Haugton.

They were seated near the top of the table.

Her father had Mrs. Langtry on one side of him and beside her was the Prince of Wales.

On his other side was the Duchess of Manchester and Flavia had read all about her in the newspapers and had seen pictures of her in *The Lady's Magazine*.

The Duchess was a great beauty and Flavia thought it was clever of her father to have the two most beautiful women in London on either side of him.

On the Earl's other side was a woman with a title whose husband was also a guest.

Although Flavia was not certain if she had read about her, she guessed that she would not be particularly young, beautiful or amusing.

Her father and Lord Carlsby were determined that the Earl should concentrate on her and it was obvious they felt that she would be thrilled to meet the most handsome man in London.

Indeed she might have been, had she not overheard their secret conversation the previous evening and if she had not been given a strict warning by her Aunt Edith.

There was, however, nothing she could do about it.

'There is no doubt,' she mused, 'that Papa has been very shrewd.'

Then she felt a little tremor run through her.

If she was to fight against him and if she was to avoid marrying the man he had chosen for her, she had to be shrewder still.

She could only hope and pray that she was strong enough, but she had to admit to feeling apprehensive.

She had brought back with her the gown she had decided to wear tomorrow night and because she had been with her aunt, she had not yet told the maid to unpack it.

Nor had she had a chance to look at her mother's jewellery her father had told her to choose from.

She rang the bell and when the butler answered, she asked him for the jewellery case from the safe.

All the jewellery that Lady Linwood had possessed, with the exception of her tiara, was kept in a large velvet-lined case and Flavia remembered, when she was a child, thinking it was very exciting.

Barker brought in the case, put it down on the sofa and then handed Flavia the keys.

"I guards that with my life, Miss Flavia," he said, "and you be careful when you've finished with it to give it back to me."

"I promise you, Barker," Flavia smiled. "But Papa wants me to wear some of Mama's jewellery tomorrow at the party and I thought it would be wise to choose it now."

"You'll look real lovely in it," Barker sighed. "Tis a pity you're too young to wear her Ladyship's tiara."

Flavia laughed.

"I'm glad I don't have to wear it. Mama always said it gave her a headache at the Opening of Parliament because it was so heavy."

"That be true, miss. But her Ladyship looked very beautiful in it and, as I often says when I sees her drive off, it be a pity she's not the Queen herself!"

Flavia laughed again.

"I'm sure that is something Mama had no wish to be. Look how worrying things have been lately and I have been feeling rather sorry for Queen Victoria."

"Oh, she'll cope with them Ruskies all right, miss. They've no wish to fight us, we be too strong and too clever for 'em and that's the truth."

Flavia agreed with Barker, but she thought it was unlucky to be too confident.

If Russia had possessed a better trained Army and it had been better organised and led, there might have been a very different story to tell about their intention to take over Constantinople.

Barker left and she carefully opened her mother's jewellery case.

Every piece of jewellery in it reminded her vividly of her mother's beauty.

However many jewels she wore, she never looked overpowered by them and they were only, as they should be, a background for her shining eyes and perfect features.

There were small and large necklaces, bracelets, rings and endless earrings.

Flavia knew that as a *debutante* it would be vulgar to wear too much jewellery and so she then chose a simple necklace of pearls and diamonds that her mother had worn when she was a girl.

There was a bracelet to match it and the only other item she took from the velvet-lined case was a star to wear in her hair.

When Barker returned to collect the case, he saw what she had chosen.

"Be that all you be going to wear, Miss Flavia?" he asked. "I do thinks, as His Royal Highness be one of the guests, you'd be shining like the sun."

Flavia giggled.

"That would be most disconcerting for everyone. After all, you must remember I am only a *debutante* from the country and so I cannot compete with all the beautiful ladies we will see here tomorrow night, like the Duchess of Manchester and, of course, Mrs. Langtry."

"Oh, her!" Barker remarked. "She's sprung up like a mushroom. If you wants to know what I thinks, she'll fall as quick as she rose!"

"I hope not – not before I've seen her."

"You'll see her everywhere, miss. They stands on the chairs in the Park to see her drive past, and there be pictures of her in all the shops. The 'Jersey Lily' they calls her and all the men, including the Prince of Wales himself, is bowled over by her."

Flavia laughed again.

"That is exactly why I am so excited at seeing her tomorrow night. Surely you are thrilled she is coming here to dinner?"

"We've been told by Mr. Wilson not to say a word about it to anyone. But I always finds when them Royals be entertained it means a lot more work and a lot more trouble!"

"But you enjoy it, Barker."

"That's as maybe, miss. There'll be Policemen and soldiers guarding the house and however much they trys to pretend no one knows, a crowd gathers outside and no one can stop 'em."

Flavia was amazed at the indignation in his voice.

"You may find all these difficulties, Barker, but I am looking forward to it because it will be wonderful for me to meet the Prince. Of course I am longing to see Mrs. Langtry too and find out if she is really as beautiful as the newspapers say she is."

When she was in the country, she had thought it extraordinary that so much could have been written about someone who had never been of any importance – then Mrs. Langtry had come to London and had attracted the attention of the Prince of Wales!

It would now be a very stupid person in any part of England who did not know who Lillie Langtry was.

*

Upstairs Mrs. Shepherd and the maids unpacked the gown Aunt Edith had chosen for Flavia.

"Now that's what I calls a very pretty gown," Mrs. Shepherd said not once but several times.

"It will give me confidence," Flavia replied. "And that I am going to need in abundance tomorrow night."

The servants were thinking that she was merely shy, which of course she was. At the same time she never for a moment forgot the reason why the party was being held – or the conniving of the two elderly courtiers who hoped they would kill 'two birds with one stone'.

She was not surprised when a message came from her father.

It was to say that he would be so late for dinner that she was not to wait for him and he would doubtless have something to eat before he finally returned.

She guessed that, having gone to see the Secretary of State for Foreign Affairs, there had been a number of other Statesmen waiting to pounce on him – she supposed she was lucky that he had not been summoned to Windsor.

As it happened, he turned up at nine o'clock.

She was still in the dining room and he sat down with her. Although he had already eaten, he had a glass of port and some *pâté* that Barker brought him.

"Cook's just finished making these, my Lord, and she feels even if you've had a good dinner you could eat a wee bit more."

"I will certainly try or cook will be disappointed."

Actually the *pâté* was so good he ate several slices and Flavia joined him.

"Now tell me what you have been doing, Flavia, and I am sure it was far more interesting than all I have had to put up with in the last few hours."

"More trouble abroad, Papa?"

"Of course, and I am afraid I will have to go down to Windsor tomorrow morning to tell the Queen about it."

Flavia wanted to say that she was sure someone else would have done that already, but she did not want to make her father feel that the Queen could do without him.

"Of course, you must go if you are summoned by Her Majesty, Papa, but you must not forget we have a party tomorrow night. His Royal Highness will be horrified if his host is not here."

"I will be here," her father promised. "Now tell me what your Aunt Edith said to you."

Flavia hesitated for a moment.

Should she tell her father that her aunt had warned her against the Earl of Haugton?

Then she thought that it might make him even more eager to tie her up quickly.

So she therefore merely told him about the clothes and who else she had met at her house and how kind they had been to her.

Also how she had been careful not to say he was holding a special dinner party for her as Aunt Edith had not been invited.

Lord Linwood put his hand up to his forehead.

"Thank goodness you have so much sense, Flavia. It was stupid of me not to tell you that I had only invited special guests who are friends of His Royal Highness."

"I did think of that, Papa."

"He will enjoy the evening more that way as he is not always at ease with strangers. Thus I chose the guests very carefully so that they will please him as well as you."

He smiled before he added,

"Actually the young men I have invited are mostly sons of his best friends. Although there are one or two who I think the Prince has not met before."

Flavia longed to ask if the Earl of Haugton had actually been introduced to him, but she thought it would be a mistake to do so.

The one thing she did not want him to realise was that she already knew a great deal about the Earl – none to his advantage.

They talked until it was time to change for dinner and then as they walked upstairs together, her father said,

"I have a charming couple coming to dinner tonight whom I know you will enjoy meeting."

"Dinner tonight!" Flavia exclaimed. "But, Papa, I thought we would be alone."

"I saw him at the Foreign Office and he said his wife was longing to meet you, so I asked them to dinner. It is impossible to squeeze them in tomorrow night and I have a feeling, although I might be wrong, that the Prince does not like him."

"I am disappointed," murmured Flavia.

"I know, my dear, but unfortunately I have to make sure that everyone of influence will do their best to make this a wonderful Season for you."

He spoke with such sincerity that Flavia could not argue and he continued,

"Lord Chatteron's wife comes from a very ancient family, who could be very useful in asking you to stay in the winter for Hunt Balls and at their Scottish Castle."

Flavia sighed.

"Must we only know people who are useful to us?"

"At the moment the answer is 'yes'. I want you to be the best success ever among the *debutantes*. And when you marry, it must be to someone who has something to offer you more than you already have at home."

She knew he was thinking of the Earl of Haugton and, as they reached the top landing, she replied,

"I know you are doing your best, Papa, to launch me, as Mama would have wanted, with all flags flying. At the same time because I love you, I want to spend as much time as I can just with you."

He kissed her.

"I feel the same, my dear, but unfortunately we both have our duties in life and mine are very demanding at present."

He did not say anything more, but walked down the corridor into his own bedroom and Flavia went into hers.

She had the feeling as she did so that the plotting and planning where she was concerned was like a net and it was closing tighter and tighter over her every minute.

She was quite certain that the two people who had been asked to dinner were friends of Lord Carlsby.

And therefore enemies of the Earl of Haugton.

Her father clearly believed that, when the time was ripe, they would be very 'useful' in his plan to rid Windsor Castle of the Earl.

Every time she thought about her situation, Flavia knew that to escape was not going to be easy.

It was a battle she might lose.

And now she had to make herself pleasant to two more people who would do anything to achieve their own objectives and they doubtless knew others they could turn to for help if it was necessary.

'But I am *alone*,' she said to herself, 'completely and absolutely alone.'

For the moment all she wanted to do was to run away to the country and, at least if she went back home, she would be safe – there would be the horses and the dogs to make her happy.

Then she told herself she would not be beaten.

Being her father's daughter put her in some way on a level with him.

Other people were outsiders and they were prepared to use her if necessary, but were not interested in her as a real person.

'I will not be defeated so easily,' she told herself. 'Even if they win, I am certain I will find a way to escape.'

Flavia went over to the window and pulled back the curtains.

When she looked out, the moon was just appearing in the darkening sky and the first star was twinkling near it.

She stood looking up at them, feeling that in some way they might help her.

Then suddenly a shooting star sped across the sky and disappeared behind the roofs of the houses.

It was almost as if the Heavens had spoken to her.

The shooting star told her there was always a way out, however frightening the future might seem.

Like the shooting star, she would somehow evade them and they would be unable to catch her.

'That is what I wanted to know,' she determined.

She threw back her head and looked up at the sky again.

"Thank you," she whispered. "Now I know that you are with me and I am no longer alone."

CHAPTER FOUR

Flavia spent the next day shopping.

Though her aunt had bought her the most beautiful dresses, she had said that she could not choose hats to match them.

"Everyone," Aunt Edith had propounded, "has an individual taste about their own hats."

Flavia spent a long time buying a great number to match her dresses. They were all striking and so different from the styles she had worn in the country.

She thought that she might be going on the stage considering the fuss made about her appearance.

Her father was continually asking her what she had chosen, if she had been to the very best shops and if she was sure that she could not do better elsewhere.

She knew at the back of his mind he was thinking that she must attract the Earl.

'If I was just thinking only of him,' she reflected, 'I would wear black and a pair of spectacles!'

She wondered what would happen if that was how she appeared at tonight's party and she was sure everyone would think she was mad and after that, they would only sympathise with her father.

She had chosen jewellery suitable for a *debutante* to wear with the gown that would have graced any stage.

She had asked her father's secretary to engage the best hairdresser in London to come to the house before dinner and arrange her hair.

As her hair was naturally curly and such a lovely golden colour she never worried about it.

She had been quite content first to brush it back from her forehead and if she was alone at home she would tie it at the back of her head with a ribbon.

Now she knew that she must do her father proud.

He was actually taking more trouble over this party than any other he had ever given and it was Mr. Wilson, his secretary, who told her that.

She wondered if at the back of his mind, he guessed the reason why, but she certainly could not ask him.

So she merely commented,

"We must not disappoint my father and I am sure you have thought of everything we could possibly need to make the evening a success."

"I do hope so," Mr. Wilson replied. "But it's very easy to forget something particularly important on these occasions. Then everything goes wrong!"

"Well, this one has to go right," said Flavia. "And I am sure it will after all the trouble you have taken."

"I have even been asked by His Royal Highness's secretary, who is a friend of mine," Mr. Wilson confided, "for a look at the guest list. It is something I have always been told is correct, but the close friends of His Royal Highness don't normally bother.

"To tell the truth, Miss Flavia, I was a little worried about the Duchess of Manchester being included."

"I have read about her and I believe that she is very beautiful."

"Very beautiful indeed," Mr. Wilson agreed, "but Her Majesty has barred her from being invited to Windsor Castle."

"She has!" Flavia exclaimed. "How extraordinary! But why?"

Mr. Wilson hesitated, obviously feeling for words.

"The Duchess," he said after a moment, "and her husband, the Duke, enjoy gambling for very high stakes. And Her Majesty has a horror of what she calls – 'the fast Manchester House Set'."

Flavia became interested as this was indeed the sort of information she could not read about in the newspapers.

"Tell me more," she begged Mr. Wilson.

"I suppose I should not really tell you, but when the Duchess was a young married woman, she attracted Lord Derby. It was whispered that under her spell he signed a promise that if he ever became Prime Minister, which was then rather unlikely, he would recommend her as Mistress of the Robes."

Flavia was listening intently and then she said,

"But Lord Derby did become Prime Minister."

"Exactly, and the Duchess made him redeem his promisory note."

Flavia was entranced.

"What happened when Queen Victoria learnt of the story?" she asked.

"She was furious and refused to send the Duchess an invitation to the Prince of Wales's wedding."

"Oh, how unkind of her! The Duchess must have been very upset."

Mr. Wilson smiled.

"She possessed a very noble name, splendid houses, great riches and a household who apparently adored her. What was more she had an iron determination."

"So she survived the insult!"

"She most certainly did. The Prince and Princess of Wales found her house parties at Kimbolton Castle and gambling *soirees* at Manchester House very much more amusing than anywhere else."

"I can quite understand why they continued to be friends," Flavia observed.

She was thinking she could understand that many people, unlike her father, found Windsor Castle very dull, especially when there were fun parties elsewhere of which Her Majesty most definitely did not approve.

"Her Grace has become very interested in politics," Mr. Wilson went on, "but one thing I admire in her is her loyalty to her friends."

"Who in particular?" Flavia enquired.

"When the Prince of Wales quarrelled with Lord Randolph Churchill and said he would enter no house that received him, the Duchess announced, 'I hold friendship higher than snobbery'."

"That was brave of her. Does she still have a great deal of power in the Prince's world?"

"A great deal," Mr. Wilson answered.

Flavia was thinking that maybe the Duchess would help her and yet she could hardly approach her without being disloyal to her father.

"I should not be talking to you about your father's friends in this manner," Mr. Wilson said. "But, as you will be meeting them all, it is useful to know 'what is what'."

"Of course it is and I am very grateful to you. Is there anything else you can tell me about the Duchess? I will certainly be thrilled to meet her this evening."

Mr. Wilson hesitated for a moment.

"Well, I suppose if I don't tell you, someone else will. The Marquis of Hartington, who will one day be the Duke of Devonshire, is madly in love with her. As he is a close friend of the Prince of Wales, you can understand that

'Harty-Tarty', as he is always called, comes into a lot of teasing and jokes about his love affairs."

"Is he coming this evening?"

"No, he is away in the country and the Duke of Manchester has refused."

"I will look forward to seeing the Duchess, but I would like to meet Lord Hartington, because I read in the newspapers that he is a great character."

"He certainly is. I heard another story about him the other day and there are a great number of them, as you will learn if you are in London for long."

"What was the one you heard?" Flavia asked him.

"He always has an answer that no one expects. A man in his railway carriage asked him if he would mind if he smoked a cigar. The Marquis answered, 'no, my dear sir, if you don't mind me being sick'!"

Flavia giggled.

"Is that the sort of answer he always gives people?"

"There is another one I heard the other day and you must forgive me, Miss Flavia, if I repeat the language he used."

"I am listening to every word," Flavia replied.

"Well, Lord Hartington was asked what he felt was the right answer to the Americans who always say when introduced, 'pleased to meet you'. He thought for a while, then he replied, 'if a fellow addressed me like that, I should say – 'so you damned well ought to be'!"

"I think that's very funny and I must tell Papa if he does not know the story already."

Mr. Wilson looked worried.

"Now don't you get me into trouble, Miss Flavia, for saying too much. I keep forgetting that you are only a *debutante*."

"I am too old to be one, as you know, but because I have read so much I find it difficult to speak like a quiet little girl who has just stepped out of the schoolroom."

Mr. Wilson laughed at this and declared,

"I am sure, Miss Flavia, that you were never any of those things, but you always made everyone aware of your looks as well as your brain, as you will tonight."

Flavia smiled at him.

"You are very encouraging and, of course, I want to be a success for Papa's sake. He has taken so much trouble over me."

She left the secretary's room, hoping that her father would be back, but there was no sign of him as yet.

She went into the ballroom to see that it was filled with flowers and was looking exceedingly attractive.

As this was only a small party, the platform for the band took up more room than usual, while a huge vase of flowers filled one end of the ballroom and made the dance floor smaller than it actually was.

'Papa thinks of everything,' Flavia thought 'and is an extremely good organiser.'

She was, however, wondering about the evening for the rest of the day.

What would the two courtiers do to make her aware of the Earl?

Perhaps they would merely assume she would fall in love with him as apparently every other young girl did.

'I will have to be very clever,' Flavia told herself. 'Otherwise I will find myself married to this horrible man! However unfaithful he might be, Papa would never forgive me if I was involved in a divorce.'

She knew that the average Society woman would go through purgatory rather than face the long drawn-out horror of a divorce which must go through Parliament.

As Flavia was dressing for dinner, her maids kept exclaiming at the beauty of her gown and how lovely she looked in it.

When she put on her mother's jewellery, she felt it gave her the strength she would need.

She finally looked at herself in the mirror and she had to admit that she really did look different from her usual self.

Every time she moved, the gown glittered and the diamond necklace encircled her neck just like protective armour against all that was waiting for her downstairs.

'I must be very brave. I must be very astute,' she told herself over and over again.

As she walked down the stairs, Barker declared,

"Oh, Miss Flavia, you do look the spitting image of your lady mother. She'd be real proud of you tonight, she would really."

"Thank you, Barker. Is his Lordship in the drawing room?"

"Indeed, miss, and Lord Carlsby is with him."

He then opened the door and to her amusement he announced,

"Miss Flavia, my Lord, the most beautiful young lady in the whole of London."

Flavia was smiling sweetly as she entered the room and joined the two gentlemen.

"Let me look at you," her father asked.

"I hope I pass the examination, Papa."

"Definitely – and with honours!"

"You look beautiful," Lord Carlsby sighed. "I am prepared to bet there is not a young lady in London who could equal, let alone beat you to the winning post!"

Flavia laughed and replied,

"I have always been told that if His Royal Highness approved of anyone, they immediately go to the top of the class."

"That is certainly true," her father said. "You must show him tonight that you are not just a small, frightened *debutante* of seventeen, who has never had an intelligent thought of her own since she left the nursery."

"If I let you down, you can send me back to the country and I will never leave the horses again!"

"There is no chance of having to do that, my dear."

As her father spoke, he put both his hands on her shoulders to show how pleased he was with her.

She noticed that he cast a glance at Lord Carlsby and clearly they were both thinking that even the spoilt and conceited Earl of Haugton would notice her.

The three of them had only been alone for a few minutes before the first guests began to arrive.

Because they were being honoured by His Royal Highness, Flavia realised that every guest had been invited either because she was beautiful, if a woman or amusing, if a man.

She could quite understand that Her Majesty Queen Victoria would be shocked if she knew about it.

This was undoubtedly one of the parties which her son would much enjoy and of which she most definitely disapproved.

Everyone complimented Flavia on her appearance.

The women, she felt, had a slightly bitter note on their lips, as if they thought – here is another contender.

While the gentlemen were sincere in saying that she was fantastic and was just what was needed in Society.

"I have never seen a duller bunch of *debutantes* than we had last year," a man said. "None of them had anything to say for themselves."

"I think you are rather sweeping, Johnnie," one of the ladies replied. "It may surprise you, but nearly every one of them was married by the end of the Season."

"Well, that is something I have no intention of doing," Flavia piped up, "until I have enjoyed London to the full. I have lived in the country for too long and now I want to see all the amusements available in this wonderful City and attend all the parties which up to now I have only read about in the newspapers."

"I promise I will help you," one of the guests said. "I will give a party for you, which will be different from all the others. Your father will tell you I have a very creative mind when it comes to entertainment."

"She has indeed," Lord Linwood agreed. "And if Doreen gives a party for you as she has promised, I know it will be sensational."

"And so will your daughter," the lady replied.

More guests were arriving all the time.

The drawing room was nearly full when the Earl of Haugton was announced.

For a moment Flavia started.

She felt as if it was impossible to move or to think.

Then, as she could see her father greeting the Earl enthusiastically, she forced herself to look at him.

He was undoubtedly one of the most handsome men she had ever seen.

He was well over six feet tall.

He had classical features and there was, she could understand, something different about him from the other gentlemen in the room.

At the same time he was her enemy and she had to fight him with every possible weapon at her disposal.

Her father was now bringing him across the room towards her.

Deliberately she turned to talk to one of the other gentleman guests and she somehow guessed that he was fond of riding.

"Tell me about your horses," she began. "I am sure that Papa told me they were exceptional."

"I would like to think so," he replied, "and I have been very fortunate in winning one or two races lately."

"It must be very exciting to see your own horse first past the winning post. To me it would be the most thrilling thing that could ever happen."

"I hope to win the Gold Cup at Ascot this year."

"I would love to see your horses before that."

"I did suggest to your father that he should bring you to luncheon one day so that you can see those I have in London. My wife and I ride in Rotten Row every morning and I expect you will be doing so too."

"I will make certain I am allowed to. My father's horses, as I expect you know, are very fine, although the best of them are in the country."

While they were talking, Flavia was aware that her father was gradually bringing the Earl nearer and nearer.

As the Earl apparently knew most of the people in the room, their progress was slow. So many either greeted him or he greeted them as they approached her.

Just as her father had almost reached her, Barker's stentorian voice was heard from the door,

"His Royal Highness the Prince of Wales and Mrs. Langtry."

There was now nothing Lord Linwood could do but hurry to the door to welcome his illustrious guests and for the moment even the Earl was forgotten.

As Flavia turned round, she stole a glance at him and yes indeed he certainly was good-looking.

Now the ladies in the party were curtsying as Lord Linwood brought the Prince and Mrs. Langtry to the centre of the room.

Then, because Flavia knew it was what her father wanted, she joined him.

"May I present, Your Royal Highness, my daughter Flavia," Lord Linwood started, "for whom this party is being given. She is as thrilled as I am that Your Royal Highness should honour us with your presence tonight."

Flavia swept down into a deep curtsy unaware how graceful she looked and just how beautifully her sparkling gown was glinting in the candlelight.

The Prince smiled at her.

"I am very delighted to meet you, Flavia," he said. "Your father is one of my oldest friends and has supported me, I might easily say, through thick and thin. Now I am determined, as I always pay my debts, to do my best for him."

"And he is most grateful, Your Royal Highness," Flavia answered. "It is marvellous for me that you are here tonight."

"I must say, having met your mother, I expected you to be beautiful. Indeed you look like a Fairy Queen who has just stepped out of Fairyland to amuse us mere mortals."

"Those are just the right words to use," a soft voice at the Prince's side remarked.

He turned to smile at Mrs. Langtry.

"I expect," he said to Flavia, "you have heard of the most glorious woman who has taken London by storm."

"I most certainly have," Flavia replied and looked towards Mrs. Langtry. "And please forgive me if I say you are far lovelier than your postcards."

Everyone laughed and Lillie Langtry added,

"That is exactly the compliment I like to receive. I thought myself the postcards were rather disappointing, but I was too polite to say so."

"How could anyone put someone as beautiful as you on a piece of paper?" the Prince of Wales asked.

She smiled at his compliment.

Flavia, watching them, thought that they were very much in love with each other.

Then Lord Linwood suggested,

"There is someone else here tonight who I want to present to Your Royal Highness and I am only surprised you have not met before. He is the Earl of Haugton."

The Prince held out his hand.

"I have heard a great deal about you," he said.

"And none of it to my advantage," the Earl replied, as he bowed.

The men laughed and Lillie Langtry commented,

"I am sure that's not true. I've been told a thousand times since I arrived in London that you were exceedingly handsome. Which of course you must know is the truth."

"I am very honoured I have been brought to your notice," the Earl replied. "At the same time I am rather afraid of becoming just one of the 'sights' of London!"

"I can give you an answer to that one," someone exclaimed, "but not when ladies are present."

The Prince laughed and so did Lord Linwood.

Flavia saw a look of satisfaction in Lord Carlsby's eyes. He obviously thought that the party was going the way he wanted.

The Prince was amused at something else the Earl said and again they were both chuckling.

Then Barker announced that dinner was served.

Lord Linwood offered his arm to the Duchess of Manchester.

Flavia had heard her announced, but had been at the other end of the room and she had therefore not been able to look at her closely.

Now, as her father led the way with her arm in his, the Prince followed with Lillie Langtry.

It was the Earl who should have taken Flavia in to dinner, but she just managed to slip her arm through Lord Carlsby's before he was aware of what was happening.

"I want you to take me in to dinner," she said, "and tell me something amusing I can say to the Prince if he speaks to me again."

Lord Carlsby smiled.

"What are his main interests?" Flavia quizzed him.

"If I am honest," he said in a voice only she could hear, "it is beautiful women. That is certainly a subject you cannot discuss in public – or in private for that matter!"

"I thought perhaps that was the answer, but His Royal Highness is much better looking than he appears in his photographs and I can understand him enjoying Social success, especially as he is not only attractive but also the Prince of Wales!"

Lord Carlsby smiled.

"And what do you think of the most handsome man in the whole country?"

Flavia forced herself to look at him in surprise.

"Who is he?" she asked innocently.

"It is the Earl of Haugton. You can hardly not have noticed him even in such a glamorous crowd as we have collected tonight for your debut."

"Oh, him! Actually I am rather disappointed."

"You don't think him handsome?" Lord Carlsby asked her in surprise.

"Not particularly. I have always believed that so much was written about him in the newspapers because they had little else to write about."

Lord Carlsby drew in his breath in surprise.

Then, as they had now reached the dining room, it was impossible for him to say any more.

Lord Carlsby escorted Flavia to her seat and went to his own on the other side of the able.

Then, as the Earl stood beside her, Flavia had an idea.

She waited until the Prince was seated with Lillie Langtry on his right and an attractive lady on his left.

Her father was now at the top of the table with the Duchess of Manchester beside him.

As the Earl sat down beside Flavia, she saw that on the other side of him was a married woman.

She had once been a beauty, but was now over fifty and she might be a friend of the Prince of Wales, but she was certainly too dull and too old for the Earl.

He would therefore have to talk to her, which was exactly what her father and Lord Carlsby planned.

Flavia drew in her breath and before the servants could start serving the first course, she rose to her feet.

She touched her wine glass with a silver spoon – it was what she had often seen her father do when he wanted to attract attention at a dinner party.

As she was standing and everyone else was sitting, they all looked up at her.

In a clear voice, which actually had a very soft and unusual sound about it, Flavia began,

"Your Royal Highness. As it is my party tonight, which is being given for me as an introduction to the gaiety and excitement of London, I want first of all to thank Your Royal Highness sincerely for coming. It is an honour that I will remember for the rest of my life."

There was a murmur of approval as she went on,

"I have, however, one request which I know Your Royal Highness will readily understand. I have been in the country in deep mourning for my Mama for a year and have seen very little of the person I love most and who I know loves me.

"To complete the wonder of this glorious party, I ask Your Royal Highness's permission for me to sit beside my father, who I have seen very little of these past months. It would so much complete my happiness and enjoyment of this wonderful evening if I can be close to him."

As she finished speaking, Flavia sat down and for a moment there was a surprised silence.

Then, as everyone clapped, the Prince said,

"Of course I will give the most beautiful *debutante* I have ever seen my permission for her to sit wherever she wishes. I am only a little peeved it's not beside me!"

Then the Duchess of Manchester rose to her feet.

"Of course I will do as this lovely girl has asked," she said. "As it so happens, I have been looking forward to making the acquaintance of the Earl of Haugton."

As the gentlemen in the party stood up, she walked round the table to take the place of Flavia.

"Thank you, thank you," Flavia enthused. "You are so kind and I knew you would understand."

"Naturally I understand, my dear, and let me tell you, you are not only the prettiest *debutante* I have seen for a long time, but certainly the best speaker."

Flavia thanked her and then she went to her father.

"I am very complimented by what you have just said, my dear," he murmured. "But it is very unusual."

"That is what I meant it to be, Papa. Anyway it is the truth. I would rather sit next to you, Papa, than anyone else."

She sensed that he was thinking that she should not have interfered with his arrangements.

But he could not put into words how anxious he had been for her to sit next to the Earl of Haugton.

As the dinner progressed and one delicious course followed another, everyone present seemed to be enjoying themselves.

There was one exception.

Lord Carlsby was scowling because, sitting exactly opposite the Earl and the Duchess, he could see that they were undoubtedly getting on well together.

The Prince was enjoying himself too.

He found it hard to take his eyes off Lillie Langtry and with the help of Lord Linwood she was making him laugh.

As Flavia knew only too well, her father could be most amusing if he wanted to be.

She had seen in the past when her mother was alive a whole table lapse into silence when he was speaking and what he said was always far more hilarious than anything they could offer themselves.

There was a charming gentleman on Flavia's other side and he was a great admirer of the Duchess and also of Benjamin Disraeli.

It was easy to make him talk about politics and he told her many things she wanted to know about the grave situation in Europe.

It was when the ladies left the dining room that he said to Lord Linwood,

"Your daughter is undoubtedly a chip off the old block, Linwood. I have had one of the most interesting conversations I have ever enjoyed at a dinner party. It is only a pity that she cannot be a boy to follow you into the House of Lords."

"I do find her equally interesting," Lord Linwood replied. "And, as you will discover, very different from the ordinary *debutantes* we have cast upon us every Season."

"She most certainly is," the man agreed. "I hope I will have the chance of talking to her again. I have the feeling that she will be besieged by young men who will be more interested in dancing with her than talking politics!"

"I will make sure she does both."

He was delighted that his daughter had been such a success with an eminent member of the Government.

After the ladies had left the dining room, they went upstairs to powder their noses and to tidy their hair.

Her mother's bedroom, which had never been used since she died, was opened as well as two other bedrooms.

They were all very kind and friendly to Flavia and when she thanked the Duchess of Manchester again for giving up her place at dinner, Her Grace replied,

"I felt I was depriving you of the most handsome man I have ever seen. As you are undoubtedly the most beautiful *debutante*, you must get together and make the most of each other."

"You were so kind to me, Your Grace, and tonight is an occasion I will always remember."

"And we will always remember you," the Duchess replied. "It was very brave of you to stand up and ask a favour from the Prince of Wales. It is what I would have done when I first came to London if I had thought of it. As it was everyone was surprised I was so outspoken. I used to say what was in my mind instead of being afraid of what people would think."

"I am sure you were right to do so," Flavia said. "I saw last year you were brave enough to attack Sir Charles Dilke when he criticised the Prussians after their defeat of France."

The Duchess laughed.

"I remember everyone was horrified with me at the time and said that I had too strong an influence on my husband."

Flavia knew that she had been gossiped about as having too strong an influence on everyone!

She wondered a little apprehensively if her father would seek the Duchess's help in forcing her to marry the Earl and then she told herself such a possibility was too far-fetched.

When the ladies came downstairs, the gentlemen then joined them.

The older members of the party sat down at the card tables while the rest headed for the ballroom.

Now the guests who had not been at dinner began to arrive. They were mostly young and were delighted with the band that Lord Linwood had engaged.

The gentlemen all admired Flavia's appearance and she next found herself dancing energetically with one after another.

They even practised 'cutting-in' when they thought one of her partners had danced with her for more than his share. They fought with each other for the next dance and Flavia found it amusing and very flattering.

It was getting on for midnight when she walked in from the garden at the back of the house.

As she tried to enter the ballroom through one of the many French windows, she found the Earl of Haugton standing in front of her.

"I have been very remiss in not asking my hostess to dance with me," he said, "but my excuse is that it has not been possible to get anywhere near her."

Flavia did not answer him and he went on,

"May I have the pleasure of this dance? I find it impossible to wait until you are without a partner."

He obviously intended to sweep away any other arrangements she had made and she was unnerved by his eagerness to dance with her.

At that very moment she was standing outside the window and he was just inside the ballroom.

Lowering her voice until it was a little more than a whisper, she said to the Earl,

"Leave me alone. It is *dangerous* – and you must ignore me."

As he stared at her in astonishment, she walked quickly past him.

She then talked animatedly to the first young man she encountered inside the ballroom.

For a moment the Earl thought he could not have heard her correctly.

There must be some mistake.

Then he saw Flavia being swept around the floor, her gown shimmering as she moved, the star in her fair hair glittering as it caught the light.

He told himself he must have imagined what she had just said to him.

It could *not* be true!

She had actually told him to ignore her.

But why?

What could be dangerous about a dance?

He stood staring at Flavia moving round the dance floor.

He thought that ever since he had come to London he had never before in his whole life had a woman tell him that it was *dangerous* for them to dance together.

Nor had any member of the female sex ever ordered him to ignore her.

CHAPTER FIVE

All the way home in his elegant carriage, the Earl was thinking about Flavia.

He had indeed expected Lord Linwood's daughter to be attractive.

He had heard many people talk about her mother.

He had accepted the invitation to the party given in Flavia's honour simply because the Prince of Wales would be there.

He was keen to meet him as he was a great admirer of the Prince and he thought, as most people did, that he was very badly treated by his mother, the Queen.

The Earl had been wondering if he should tell the Queen that many people felt she was being exceedingly unkind to her eldest son.

Then he told himself it was none of his business.

At any rate he would wait till he had met the Prince which would give him a better idea of whether the Queen was right or wrong.

The Earl was a very positive person and considered himself an excellent judge of character.

He believed it was wrong that the Prince of Wales was not allowed to take any part in affairs of State.

However, as he was very astute, he always thought before he did anything unusual and he had no intention where Her Majesty was concerned of putting a foot wrong.

Because he had spent so much time at Windsor Castle with those who were actively engaged in attending on the Queen, he had never before been to a party where the Prince of Wales was the chief guest.

He was also much flattered that the Queen should consult him on so many different matters and it was quite obvious that she really enjoyed his company.

He thought she was really 'a nice old girl', but she was the Queen of the United Kingdom and he was totally fascinated by all the pomp and ceremony with which she was surrounded.

Ever since childhood the Earl had more or less been in command of his own home and those who served in it.

His mother had died when he was at school at Eton and his father had, when he came home, practically handed over the running of the estate to him.

It was an extraordinary situation for a young boy to find himself in, although, since most of those employed on the estate had been there for years, they advised him in the correct manner.

They also accepted the fact that as his father was no longer interested in the estate and thus his son, Vincent, however inexperienced, had to take his place.

Actually, after his mother's death, his father was seldom at home and spent much of his time travelling in Europe.

In the meantime, Vincent struggled on at home and learnt cannily to turn everything to his own advantage.

He entertained his closest friends from school and they enjoyed riding his horses, shooting his pheasants, and helping him organise races and steeplechases.

It was not surprising that everyone at Eton and later at Oxford University moved Heaven and earth to be invited to Haugton Hall.

Thus Vincent became the most popular student at both places.

At Eton he did very well at cricket and followed it up by being made Captain of the Christ Church College cricket team at Oxford.

If there is one talent the British admire the most, it is a man who is good at games.

And so it was not surprising that the young Vincent became a most sought after and flattered young man when he first appeared on the Social scene.

Yet, from the moment he finished his education, he was determined to travel.

He sought out his father and learnt from him about the countries that up to now had just been names on maps, and then his father gave him introductions to the Rulers of countries he was interested in.

It was not surprising, with such a varied education and having been a success wherever he went, that when he became the tenth Earl of Haugton on his father's death, the Social world welcomed him enthusiastically.

By this time, Vincent had discovered women – or rather women had discovered *him*.

Because he was so exceptionally good-looking and boasted an ancient title, women pursued him from the time he left Eton.

At first he was not particularly interested in them, but he learnt a great deal about the female sex when he was in France on an extended visit.

In other countries he visited, it was accepted that he should find it easy to make love to the most beautiful of the women at Court – and there was a great variety of them.

Then when he eventually came home to England, he was introduced by one of his relatives to the Queen at Windsor Castle.

He found that she not only admired him for his looks, as she always liked handsome men, but Her Majesty was really interested in his knowledge of foreign countries.

She found his reports fascinating and useful and she took a rather perverse pride in keeping one step ahead of her Statesmen – she really enjoyed knowing more about some Eastern Potentates than they did.

The Earl realised that she was picking his brains and was only too delighted to encourage her to do so and he was not in the least bit shy of expressing his opinions to Her Majesty.

Many found Queen Victoria overwhelming and so were afraid to contradict her on any subject.

They would have been surprised if they had known how she listened attentively to everything the Earl told her and invariably asked for more.

Of course, as soon as he appeared in London at the start of the Season, he was bombarded with invitations from every fashionable hostess and ambitious mother.

He knew he was a great catch in the matrimonial market. However, he had long ago decided that he would not be caught.

He was well aware when he reached his twenty-seventh birthday that most of his contemporaries both at Eton and Oxford were married and the majority of them had started a family.

This was often because they had inherited a title or were going to inherit one and so most of them had been pushed up the aisle by their pushy relations.

The Earl enjoyed pretty women, of course he did, and there were a great number to choose from.

Unfortunately he found that his *affaires-de-coeur* never lasted long. Inevitably after a few weeks he began to feel restless and bored by conversations that never varied.

There was no doubt that there was little more he could say about love than he had said already.

Exciting and fiery, it was always marvellous when it started, but, where he was concerned, it died down too quickly and it faded away into a boredom that he could not ignore.

Sometimes he noticed a beautiful woman whom he thought completely and utterly desirable.

She would look at him across a ballroom with an invitation in her eyes, but he would be aware that a number of men were fighting for her attention.

It was then he thought that there must be something wrong with him and when he diagnosed it, he found the answer was always the same.

The lovely creatures appealed *only* to his body!

He would be the very first to admit that they were highly successful at doing so – but not to his mind.

Only occasionally did he have a conversation with a beauty that did not concern herself.

Inevitably, he found that he was talking to a woman who was not really listening to what he was saying and instead she was wondering just how soon he would kiss her again.

"The trouble with women," he had said to one of his friends recently, "is that they are too eager and one does not really have to make much effort to win them."

His friend had laughed.

"That is what you may think, Vincent, because you are exceptional. But poor creatures like myself who do not have your good looks or your possessions, have to wait for what we want or find when we do knock on the door it is closed against us!"

"That's a very sad story," the Earl commented.

"But it happens to be true," his friend answered. "And you should be thankful for being the exception. No woman refuses you and that is what we resent about you."

The Earl had chuckled, but he had not denied that was it the truth.

Yet now, for the first time in his life, a woman was avoiding him and actually telling him to ignore her!

As he had entered the drawing room this evening and had seen Flavia, he had thought she was exceptionally lovely and she seemed so unlike the other women present in a way he could not explain.

Then he saw her name next to his on the dining room table and considered that he was very lucky to be sitting next to her on such an auspicious occasion.

She was certainly beautiful in a different way from the other beauties present.

He could not quite explain it or put it into words.

But he thought she was unique to look at, although doubtless, as she was so young, she would have little to say for herself.

Then to his surprise, she had risen to her feet and, without showing any shyness had made a speech, asking the Prince of Wales if she could change her place at the table so that she could be near her father whom she loved.

The Earl thought that she spoke brilliantly for such a young girl.

He also thought it exceptionally brave of her to rise and address the Prince of Wales without apparently any prior arrangement.

When His Royal Highness then agreed and Flavia changed places with the Duchess of Manchester, the Earl was taken aback.

At the same time he did not suppose that there was anything personal about her wish to change her place.

But then he had asked her politely to dance and she had answered him in such an astonishing manner.

He could only think that something had happened, which he did not know about and he could not think what it could possibly be.

Why should knowing her be dangerous?

The words seemed to repeat themselves in his ears over and over again as he drove home.

Even when he got into bed, he found it impossible not to hear her whisper,

"Leave me alone. It is dangerous – and you must ignore me."

The Earl made up his mind before he went to sleep that he must find out the reason for this rebuff, but equally he could not think how.

After all Lord Linwood had always been pleasant to him when they had met at Windsor Castle and the same might be said of Lord Carlsby.

He remembered that another elder Statesman, when he had first started to visit the Queen several times a week, had said to him,

"You are now popular with Her Majesty and have become a privileged person at Windsor, but don't upset Lords Linwood and Carlsby, who have been Her Majesty's closest advisers for some considerable time."

"I have no wish to upset anyone," he had replied.

He had not really thought again about the warning.

He was, however, more than a little surprised when Lord Linwood had invited him to a small and intimate dinner party.

He said he was giving it for his daughter as soon as she arrived in London, a party that the Prince of Wales had already agreed to attend.

If it had been a large ball, such as he was invited to every night and to which the members of the *Beau Monde* seemed to attend automatically, he would have accepted it as perfectly normal.

Of course, as the Earl of Haugton, he was on the list of all the fashionable hostesses and at the age of twenty-seven he was well aware of his own attractions – not the least being his bank balance.

He might, however, have expected Lord Linwood's invitation simply because he was persona grata at Windsor Castle and if Lord Linwood did resent the attention the Queen was giving him, he made no sign of it.

The Prince of Wales was very different and the Earl had been surprised when, as the ladies left the dining room, Lord Linwood had told him with a gesture of his hand to sit down next to the Prince.

Being naturally a wit, he had found it easy to make the Prince laugh and when it was time to join the ladies, His Royal Highness had declared,

"You must come to Marlborough House, my boy. I know all your stories that have entertained me this evening will amuse my friends."

"That is very kind of Your Royal Highness," the Earl replied. "I will be delighted and very honoured to be a guest at Marlborough House."

"I expect you have heard of the alterations I have been making to it. I was told, I think it must have been by Linwood, that you have made some major improvements recently at Haugton Hall."

"I have altered the picture gallery and bought some

very fine pictures recently in Rome that I would like Your Royal Highness to view."

He paused, wondering if he had said too much and the Prince would consider that he was being too pushy.

But the Prince had smiled at him and responded,

"I would really love to see them and so would Mrs. Langtry. If you have a date when you would like to invite us, discuss it with my private secretary. I would be most interested not just to see your pictures but Haugton Hall too."

The Prince with Lord Linwood then led the way from the dining room and by the time the Earl had reached the ballroom, the Prince was dancing with Mrs. Langtry.

The Earl felt it was only polite that he should ask the Duchess of Manchester for a dance as he had sat next to her at dinner.

She was a superb dancer and, as they swept round the room to a romantic waltz, she asked,

"What do you think of our host's daughter? She is really lovely."

"I find most young girls," replied the Earl, "have little to say for themselves. I was impressed, however, that she made that speech which was apparently unprompted, but naturally I did enjoy sitting with you and having that most fascinating conversation."

"Now you are flattering me," the Duchess smiled. "But I enjoyed our conversation too. It was an entirely serious political one, but I don't reproach you for that!"

The Earl laughed as he knew only too well about the Duchess's reputation and she seldom talked to a man without flirting with him.

They had in fact plunged into a conversation over the new Education Bill as the Duchess was supporting the proposer of the Bill, Mr. William Forster, who was one of her close friends.

As he expected, the Queen was violently against anything that the Duchess approved of and naturally she disliked the Duchess, not only for her political convictions, but because of her gambling and her attraction for men.

The Earl had enjoyed every moment of his dinner. Everything she said to him was exactly what he wanted to know about influence and lobbying at Windsor.

Nevertheless later in the evening he realised he had not behaved correctly and asked to dance with his hostess – or rather the *debutante* the dinner was given for.

When he had approached Flavia, he had expected her eyes to reproach him for being so slow in requesting a dance.

Her answer had been as astonishing as if she had fired a pistol at him.

*

He had woken in the morning no less determined to find an explanation.

He was not quite certain where to begin.

Thinking it over, he came to the conclusion that his best idea would be to call at Linwood House.

He would leave a bouquet of flowers for Flavia and a letter thanking Lord Linwood for his hospitality.

It had truly been a most enjoyable and interesting dinner party and he had actually enjoyed himself more than at any other party this Season.

He had, with an invitation to Marlborough House, definitely set off on the right foot.

'Why,' he wondered, 'must I *ignore* Flavia?'

It was quite obvious from what everyone else had said last night that Flavia Linwood would be the 'belle' of the Season.

Then why, why, why did he have to ignore her?

What could the danger be?

If there were two things the Earl found fascinating, they were a problem he could not solve at once and the unexpected.

He knew he must find an answer to this dilemma.

He sat down and wrote his letter of thanks and then he ordered the flowers and a carriage for three o'clock.

He was then aware that his secretary and his butler were looking at him in some surprise that he was attending to his correspondence first thing after breakfast.

The horse he was to ride that morning in Rotten Row was waiting for him at the door. It was one of his latest purchases and a superb thoroughbred.

He knew when he was riding it that there was no one in Rotten Row or anywhere else in London, for that matter, who could equal him.

He set off, enjoying the sunshine and the fresh air, which was sweeping in from the trees in Park Lane.

It was when he was halfway down Rotten Row that he saw Lord Linwood coming towards him. He was riding a very fine horse and beside him was Flavia.

The Earl had to admit she looked almost as smart and sensational in an attractive riding habit as she had done last night in her glittering gown.

As they met face to face, the Earl swept off his hat and spoke to Lord Linwood,

"Good morning. I have just written a letter to you to thank you for a most stimulating evening. In fact I have never enjoyed myself more."

"I am so delighted," Lord Linwood answered him, "and I understand you are inviting His Royal Highness to Haugton Hall."

"His Royal Highness was kind enough to say that he would like to see some pictures I bought in Rome when I was last there."

"I am hoping that, when he does come, you and Miss Flavia will also honour me."

"We will be enchanted," said Lord Linwood. "Do arrange your party as soon as possible."

"I will most certainly do so," the Earl answered and looked towards Flavia.

She was frowning at him.

Her forehead was definitely wrinkled and he knew without her saying it that she did not want to accept his invitation.

The Earl was wondering what he could do, when Lord Linwood remarked,

"Ah, there is Lady Brentford. I must have a word with her."

He then moved his horse quickly towards one of the open carriages that had drawn up at the side of the Row so that those occupying it could talk both to those riding and people walking on the footpath.

The Earl realised that he and Flavia were for the moment left behind.

He rode closer to her.

"I must see you," he began. "I want to ask you for an explanation of what you said to me last night."

"Just leave me alone," Flavia blurted out. "Pay no attention to me and you must *not* come to the house."

She spoke quickly and at that moment a man riding a spirited horse that was bucking a bit came up beside her.

"That was a marvellous party you gave last night, Miss Linwood," the man began. "I hope you will save me a dance at the Beaufort's party tonight. I am sure you will be one of the guests."

Flavia smiled at him.

"I must ask Papa, but I expect we are going. He said something about it yesterday."

"Then please promise me the first dance and a great number of dances after that," the man blustered on.

Flavia laughed.

"You must not be greedy. As I have just arrived in London, there are a great number of people I want to meet, who up to now have just been names to me in *The Court Circular*."

The young man chuckled.

"I suppose I should be grateful I am grand enough to be in it. Do I get my dance?"

"It depends what time you arrive," Flavia answered. "If you are late and my dance card is full, what can I do about it?"

"I think you are being very unkind," the young man protested and turned to the Earl.

"What do you think, Vincent?" he asked.

Before the Earl could answer, Flavia moved away and she was now riding quickly down Rotten Row, passing her father who was still talking to his friend in the carriage.

The Earl felt that he should follow her and then changed his mind.

'I must get to the bottom of this,' he determined.

But for the moment he could not see how.

Hoping to avoid the Earl, Flavia rode to the end of Rotten Row and waited for her father to join her.

When he did so, he asked her quizzically,

"Why did you hurry away so quickly? I thought you would be pleased to talk to the Earl."

"I did not get the chance, Papa. A rather tiresome man, who pursued me last night, came up and started to ask for a dozen dances or so at the Beaufort's party tonight. As I have no wish to dance even one dance with him, the only thing I could do was to gallop away."

Lord Linwood was frowning.

"I hope you were not rude to the Earl, my dear. He was a great success with the Prince of Wales last night and I would indeed like to visit Haugton Hall when His Royal Highness is also a guest."

Flavia did not answer and, after they had ridden on a little way, Lord Linwood added,

"I thought he was more pleasant than I expected him to be and the Duchess was saying the most flattering words about him."

Flavia did not reply and yet she realised that her father was waiting for her to say something.

"I think the party was a huge success, Papa," she answered after what seemed a long pause, "and everyone said how much they enjoyed themselves. If you are not careful, you will find you will have to give another party."

"Which I have every intention of doing. The only difficulty will be to find a vacant evening when we are not going somewhere else."

"I saw a large number of letters arrive just before we left the house. Of course they may have been bills!"

Her father laughed.

"If they are, I will settle them all. But you were a great success and I was very proud of you last night."

They rode on for a little while before he added,

"It was very sweet of you to want to sit with me at dinner, but I really wanted you to get to know the Earl."

"But I have no wish to know him, Papa."

"Why ever not?"

"He is too busy with women like the Duchess of Manchester and Aunt Edith told me he has little use for unmarried girls, especially *debutantes*."

Lord Linwood scowled.

"That is absolute nonsense! You must not believe anything your aunt tells you about anyone as she always exaggerates."

"There are lots of charming men in London besides the Earl," she responded, "so don't let's bother about him."

She realised that her father's lips had tightened and he was preventing himself from saying all he really wanted to say.

He therefore changed the subject and, as Flavia was so astute, she managed to make her father laugh before they arrived back in Grosvenor Square.

*

However, later on in the day, a beautiful bouquet of orchids arrived at the house and her father said that he had received a charming letter from the Earl.

She now realised that she would have to tell the Earl sooner or later why they must not associate with each other, and she wondered if she should write him a letter of thanks for the bouquet.

Later in the afternoon she was sitting alone in the library reading a book.

Her father had gone to see the Prime Minister and had promised he would be back for tea even if he was late.

Because they were going out in the evening, Flavia had no wish to go shopping and anyway she thought that she had enough clothes to last her for a year or more.

She was enjoying a book about the reign of Charles II when Barker entered.

"There's a note for you, Miss Flavia," he said, "and the messenger's waiting for an answer."

She took the letter from the proffered silver salver and she sensed that she knew who it was from even before she opened it.

It was short and to the point.

"*I have to have an explanation for what you said to me last night and again this morning.*

I will meet you at any place at any time you suggest where we will not be seen."

It was not signed and there was no address at the top of the writing paper.

Flavia felt the moment had come when she had to answer him.

They could hardly go on as they were and it could be very threatening if he was not aware that he must play his part in the charade as well as she was doing.

"I will send an answer," she said to Barker. "Please come back in five minutes."

Barker bowed and left the room.

Flavia went to her father's writing table in the next room.

She wondered if it would be possible for them to sit in separate rooms and she could whisper to him through the secret shelf.

Then she knew that it was impossible, as it was so important for him not to come to the house.

Because she was intelligent, she suddenly thought of a solution that would not have occurred to anyone else.

"*Please meet me,*" she wrote, "*in the Gallery of the Grosvenor Chapel tomorrow morning.*

If you are there at eleven o'clock, I will arrive at eleven-fifteen."

She did not sign her name nor did she address the envelope.

She merely rang the bell and told Barker to take it to the waiting messenger.

"I don't know who he is, Miss Flavia," Barker said, "and when I asked him who the letter were from, he were most cheeky and told me to mind me own business."

He was obviously affronted by such impertinence and Flavia wanted to laugh.

Instead of which she told Barker,

"It is from someone who wants to meet me without anyone knowing. He is a married man and, of course, I have told him to leave me alone."

"I thinks it be sommat like that," Barker muttered.

"You are not to tell His Lordship, Barker, for the simple reason it would upset him, as you well know."

"Me lips be sealed, miss."

Barker took the note and carried it outside.

Flavia sat making her plans.

It was not going to be easy, but at least it was very unlikely anyone would see her.

She had often been to the Grosvenor Chapel when she was a child and she had enjoyed sitting in the Gallery rather than being in the usual pew with her mother.

"I cannot think why you want to be upstairs in the Gallery," her mother had commented.

"I was reading, Mama, that in the East the higher they made their religious buildings, the nearer they thought they were to God."

"That's a very good excuse," my dear, "for wanting to look down on the people below and seeing them from an angle at which no one sees oneself!"

"That's a good explanation, Mama, and far better than any I can think of."

"Very well," her mother conceded. "When we go to the Chapel, you will sit in the Gallery and I am sure your father will much prefer a pew down below."

A compromise was agreed that, when her father was there, they sat in the family pew and when he was not, her nanny or her mother escorted Flavia up to the Gallery.

*

She was only hoping there was not a Service taking place tomorrow morning.

Her father went off early, because he had to go to Windsor Castle, promising to return in time for tea.

Flavia had the feeling he wanted to report to Lord Carlsby how badly they had progressed with regard to the Earl – and probably to see the Queen and find out the latest developments in the troubles with Russia.

'One thing that will please him,' Flavia thought, 'the Earl will not be at the Castle this morning when he is there.'

She told the housekeeper that she wanted to buy a few items from the shops in South Audley Street and that she would like Molly to go with her.

Molly was an old housemaid, who had been in her father's service for over forty years.

She had refused to retire because she had no home to go to nor did she have any relations who would offer her one. She was going blind and suffered from arthritis in her knees.

"Why do you want Molly?" asked Mrs. Shepherd. "You know she's getting too old to do anything but just sit about."

"Molly has been with us longer than anyone else," Flavia insisted, "and I would not like her to think she is ignored because she is old, which will happen to us all."

She and Molly set out.

They walked slowly while Molly told her what a beautiful baby she had been and how much she had loved her mother.

"A kinder lady never left this world," she said in all sincerity," and if anyone be in Heaven, it be her."

"I agree with you, Molly. That is why I am going to the Chapel today where you recall I went when I was small and I am going to say a special prayer for Mama."

"That's just what you should do, miss. You can be sure your mother will hear it wherever she be."

It took some time to reach the Grosvenor Chapel in South Audley Street and the doors were open.

Flavia could see that there was no one in the lower part of the Church.

"I am going up to the Gallery," she said to Molly. "But you are to stop down here and not try to walk up those narrow stairs."

"They be too much for me," Molly admitted.

"I thought so," said Flavia. "I will just say a prayer then I will come back to you."

The old maid moved into one of the pews at the back of the Church, as Flavia hurried up the stairs to the Gallery.

When she reached the top, she looked round and for a moment she thought that the Earl was not there.

Then she saw him at the very back of the Gallery and he was the only person present.

She moved along the back row of seats until she reached him.

He did not rise as if he thought that it might draw attention to them, although there was no one in sight.

As she sat down beside him, he began,

"It's clever of you to think of this. There is no one to see us here."

"Touch wood," she exclaimed, "but I remembered that eleven o'clock is not a fashionable time."

"You realise I had to see you," the Earl said. "I could hardly go on worrying night and day over what you said."

Flavia smiled.

"I don't believe it's worrying you as much as that."

"I hate a puzzle I cannot solve," he replied almost petulantly. "I cannot understand what is going on and I assure you it's giving me sleepless nights."

"Very well, I'll tell you the truth and perhaps you will think of a better solution than mine."

"I certainly hope so, Flavia."

Then slowly and quietly in case her voice should carry, Flavia told him all she had overheard her father and Lord Carlsby saying that night when she had left the dining room.

"I did not know there were holes in the bookcase," Flavia added, "but when I heard my name mentioned, I listened."

"Of course you did," the Earl agreed. "But I had no idea that your father and Lord Carlsby thought that I was undermining their position at Court when I talked with the Queen."

"You must have upset them quite a lot."

The Earl smiled.

"Only because I made suggestions which had not been thought of before and I did not think for a moment that Her Majesty took them seriously."

"She certainly discussed them with Papa and Lord Carlsby and they thought you were interfering. Everyone has told me that if Her Majesty gets an idea into her head, nothing will make her change it, except of course someone like *you*."

The Earl wanted to laugh but prevented himself.

"Do you really believe," he asked "that your father would agree to you being pushed into marriage with me, rather than lose what he believes to be his control over the Queen?"

"It sounds somewhat unpleasant put like that, but you know as well as I do that people consider you a great Social catch. So my father would think I was very lucky if I married you and I should jump at the chance. But you will understand I much prefer to choose my own husband."

"As I want to choose my own wife, if I ever take one!"

"Well, we agree on that, if nothing else."

"We agree on everything. I think you have been exceedingly clever and have done the only possible thing you could have done under the circumstances."

Flavia smiled at him.

"Thank you, kind sir, for your considerate words."

"No, I am serious. It was a terrible predicament to find yourself in and you have dealt with the situation very astutely. What we have to decide now is just how we will manage to avoid being caught out in circumstances which they can claim are compromising."

Flavia gave a sigh.

"That is what I hoped you would say. It has been so worrying being pushed onto you by Papa and I cannot be expected to change my seat at *every* party!"

"We will have to talk this over again some time or another," the Earl suggested.

"We can come here, but if we do, the servants will think that I have suddenly become very religious and they will talk about it in the servants hall, if nowhere else."

"Servants! Servants!" the Earl cried. "They have changed the course of history more often than people are ever aware."

Flavia gave a little giggle.

"That is true. So what are we going to do?"

"I will think of something, but, of course, we can come here occasionally, if things are desperate. If I send a note with just a time on it, you will know what I mean."

"And I will do the same, but we will have to leave the notes somewhere, otherwise our staff are bound to talk, and if we carry on avoiding each other, then Papa may get suspicious."

"I think that Lord Linwood and Lord Carlsby are fussing quite unnecessarily. I would hate to just disappear from Windsor Castle and leave the Queen wondering what had upset me."

"No, of course you cannot do that. It must be very nice for Her Majesty to have someone young and of course *handsome*, to talk to."

She exaggerated the word handsome and he said,

"If you tease me too much about that, I will grow a beard, wear dark glasses and dye my hair white!"

"That would be sensational and would doubtless cause headlines in the newspapers."

"No seriously," the Earl protested, "I am sick of people going on about my looks, while naturally you are only too willing to listen to people eulogising about yours."

"I am delighted that people think I am pretty. It would be awful if I was so plain no one ever noticed me!"

"I suppose you are right, Flavia, and we should be grateful for small mercies."

"I think these are particularly big ones. The trouble is that it gives my father ideas and it is doubtless tedious for you that all the ambitious mothers pursue you."

"Not because of my looks, but because of my title. I assure you that I have no wish to marry anyone, *including you.*"

"I can say exactly the same," asserted Flavia. "But I expect we will both be trapped sooner or later and the best solution is to avoid it for as long as possible."

"If you talk like that," the Earl said, "I will leave England immediately and go to Timbuktu or perhaps one of the deserts I have not yet visited. The Arab women, I assure you, keep their faces and themselves well hidden!"

Flavia giggled again.

"Don't make me laugh, as my maid, although a little deaf, might hear me."

"Did you bring a maid with you, Flavia?"

"Of course I did. I am a young lady and I therefore have to be chaperoned."

"I had forgotten that piece of protocol. How would you like to roam over the desert or the mountains of Tibet without anyone to bother about you?"

"It is the sort of venture that will never be possible unless I was with my husband," replied Flavia. "I assure you that I would then enjoy it enormously."

"One day perhaps I will be able to tell you about it and how wonderful it is, but now it looks unlikely that we will be able to have a sensible conversation of any sort."

"It's a subject I would so love to hear about and I have read a great number of books about it. I would love to go to Tibet and, if you ask me my greatest ambition, I would like to be the first woman to climb Mont Blanc."

He began to laugh, then quickly stopped himself by putting his hand over his mouth.

"That's not the right answer," he smiled. "What you should really be saying, as a nicely brought up young lady, is that you wish to marry a Marquis or a Duke and open a Flower Show every day for the rest of your life!"

It was Flavia's turn to stop herself from laughing out loud.

"Can you think of anything more boring? But I imagine most young women who are making their debut at the moment would think it the nearest thing to Heaven."

"Of course they would," he agreed, "and perhaps the only way we could escape from being married without our consent is to run away to one of the places where no white man or woman has ever been before."

Flavia sighed.

"That is what *you* can do only too easily, but I am unfortunately a woman and therefore I have to obey the conventions, whether I like it or not."

"Of course you must. And you must help me to be clever enough not to be caught in this very uncomfortable whirlpool which I now know is threatening me."

"If you send me a letter, don't give it to a servant, just address it to me," Flavia suggested, "and then drop it through the letter box, preferably when no one is looking."

"I will do that, but how can you communicate with me?"

Flavia thought for a moment.

"I have just thought of a better way for both of us. There is a statue in the gardens of Grosvenor Square. I noticed when I was looking at it yesterday that a heel of the statue has cracked and it would be quite easy to slip a note underneath it."

The Earl nodded and she continued,

"When you are passing this way, just go into the gardens. Then look under the heel at the foot of the statue to see if I have left anything there for you."

The Earl smiled.

"I will and leave my note for you there."

"That will make it exciting for me – "

"You are very clever and I am beginning to suspect this is a game that will amuse us for some time to come."

Flavia was silent for a moment and then she said,

"To be married to someone you don't love is not at all amusing! Remember if we are caught in what they will call a compromising situation, as they intend us to be, it will be impossible for either of us to object to becoming publicly engaged or else cause a fearful scandal."

"You are right, Flavia, we must take this seriously."

"Indeed we must, but at this very moment we are laughing at it. And if you are forced to take me as your wife, you will *not* be laughing, nor will I."

The Earl looked at her.

"That is a funny thing for you to say. I have always thought that all the women I met longed to marry me and it was only I who was in opposition to the idea."

"I assure you that I have no wish to marry you or anyone else I don't love," Flavia insisted. "I will be very critical and suspicious of anyone who says he loves me."

She spoke earnestly and the Earl was thinking she looked very lovely.

Then he held out his hand and took hers.

"I promise you that I will play this game seriously and we must both contrive with everything in our power to outwit those who are threatening us."

Flavia took her hand from his.

"Thank you, now please wait for five minutes while I collect my old maid and walk away.

"I think ten minutes will be safer," the Earl replied. "I am not in the habit of dropping in here and anyone who sees me coming out of the Chapel might think it strange."

"You are so clever, you think of everything," Flavia said. "That was stupid of me."

"You have been very canny so far and good luck in the future."

"And the same to you."

Then she rose and left him.

As he heard her footsteps going down the stairs, he reflected that never in his whole life had he been in such an extraordinary situation.

Nor had he ever had a partner who was so beautiful, at the same time so out-spoken and definitely intelligent.

As he thought of Lord Linwood and Lord Carlsby, he smiled.

'We will now give the old gentlemen a run for their money,' he told himself. 'It will certainly be something new and a situation I could never have expected in my wildest dreams.'

CHAPTER SIX

Flavia found herself overwhelmed with invitations.

She had to consult her father as to which ones she should accept and he was most helpful by describing his friendship or association with each hostess.

She attended three very large balls and to her relief the Earl was not at any of them.

Equally she could not help thinking it was much more amusing talking to him than with any of the young gentlemen she danced with.

They were either the same age or only a little older than she and after they had paid her fulsome compliments, she found there was really very little else to talk about.

Some were in the Army but posted only in London Barracks and others had been studying at University and none of them had travelled.

People she was really interested in were those who had visited far-off countries she hoped one day to see.

However, to please her father she made herself as pleasant as she could.

At the end of the week she confided in him,

"I have had two proposals of marriage, Papa, and another is only on the horizon at the moment but is coming nearer every day."

Her father looked surprised.

Even before he spoke she knew he was worried that she might accept someone other than the Earl.

"You should not be in a hurry," he replied after a moment's silence. "You must remember, my dear, that the man you marry will be with you for the rest of your life. Therefore you have to be very sure that he is the right one before you accept him."

"That is just what I have thought, Papa, and when I remember how happy you and Mama were, I knew at once that I would never be happy with any of the men who have proposed to be."

"Of course, I also want you to make an important marriage," he added.

She realised at once that he was thinking of the Earl and answered him innocently,

"Do you mean me to marry someone with a title?"

"Of course I do. I want you to marry someone of importance socially, who has an estate as large as our own and naturally outstanding horses."

Flavia realised that he was describing the Earl very accurately, so she responded,

"I don't think I know anyone like that. In fact the gentlemen who asked me to dance last night all had healthy fathers who are not likely to pass on their Coronets, if they have one, for another forty or fifty years!"

Lord Linwood laughed as if he could not help it.

"I hope it will not be as bad as that, my dear, but the eldest son of a Peer is always someone of significance. As you are so exceptionally beautiful, I feel that only the very best is good enough for you."

Flavia's eyes were twinkling as she answered,

"You must really be thinking about the Prince of Wales, Papa. But he, as we both know, is married with five children!"

He laughed again.

"I was not referring to the Prince of Wales, but when he was a young man he was undoubtedly the greatest catch in the matrimonial calendar."

"I think Princess Alexandra must be a Saint to put up with the way he goes on now."

She was recalling how engrossed he was with Mrs. Langtry and she felt that, if her husband behaved like that, she would be extremely angry.

"The Prince of Wales is a law unto himself," Lord Linwood continued. "What I am thinking about, my dear, is that you should have the best of life in the future and I hope that when you do fall in love, which you undoubtedly will, it will be with a gentleman of title and authority, who will look after you when I am no longer here."

Flavia longed to say that the people she needed to be protected from were him and Lord Carlsby!

Instead she declared innocently,

"I am sure, Papa, that this wonderful suitor will fall down from Heaven eventually. But I assure you up to now I have not met him."

She knew that he was longing to contradict her, but he was too wise to do so.

She kept wondering what would be the next step he and Lord Carlsby would take to bring the Earl and herself together.

*

For the moment he seemed to have disappeared out of her world and she suspected that, when her father came back from Windsor short-tempered and disagreeable, that the Earl was stirring things up there with the Queen.

Every day she made the same excuse to go into the Square.

She looked eagerly to see if there was a message for her under the statue.

By a stroke of luck she had found out Mr. Wilson had a dog.

When her father was in residence, he was left at home, but otherwise Mr. Wilson brought him to his office.

"Bracken is very good," he told Flavia. "I take him for a run either in the garden or into the Square. He meets dogs there who belong to other residents and, as he is such a very friendly creature, they never fight."

"I must see him," said Flavia. "So please bring him in every morning when you come to do our letters. I will take him for a run, so that you don't feel you are wasting Papa's time."

Mr. Wilson was delighted at the idea, as she knew he had worried because he had to leave his dog for many hours alone in his small flat.

It was an excellent excuse for going into the Square with Bracken and while he enjoyed himself with the other dogs, she looked eagerly under the foot of the statue.

This was now the fourth day since she had talked with the Earl.

She thought that, if there was nothing there for her soon, it would be very disappointing.

She had been enjoying the intrigue, even though it was serious, with a man who was a good bit older than her.

The young men she danced with were all brainless and the Earl played the 'game', as he called it, with a quick intelligence.

She had hoped to see him in Rotten Row.

But, after the first day they had met there, he had not appeared again.

She had the idea he either went much earlier in the morning or to another part of the Park and it was somehow disappointing when he did not come riding towards her.

He looked, she had to admit, magnificent on one of his superb thoroughbreds.

She went first to Mr. Wilson's office.

"Good morning, Miss Flavia," he said. "There is another pile of invitations for you and I am prepared to bet that no other *debutante* has ever received so many in such a short time!"

"I feel sure that Papa will be gratified. I am just wondering if every ball I go to will always be exactly the same as the previous one."

Mr. Wilson looked at the pile in front of him.

"I cannot promise you anything unusual, but I have not opened all the post as yet."

"I will take Bracken for a walk. Perhaps amongst that pile there is an invitation to something I have not yet done."

"I am sure there will be," Mr. Wilson replied.

But she knew he was only being polite and she had actually, although she did not say so, found last night's ball rather dull.

It was exactly the same as the ball she had attended the night before and the night before that.

There had been the same young men at dinner and on one side of her there was an Honourable and on the other a Viscount.

They were both at University and their conversation was exclusively on sport.

The Viscount talked about cricket and she learnt he was a good bowler and the Honourable was taking part in the Boat Race between Oxford and Cambridge.

The other young gentlemen she danced with were all replicas of one another.

At the end of the evening she found it was difficult to remember their names or to be the slightest concerned as to whether she would meet them again.

'I would so much rather be with Papa,' she decided. 'At least we can talk about politics, the Russian menace or what is happening in France.'

Then she told herself it was no use being critical as she had to accept what was on offer and be thankful for it.

Bracken was delighted to be taken for a walk and although Flavia put him on a lead, he jumped and twisted and attempted to run ahead of her.

When she reached the Square, she released Bracken because she knew he would not go far and he was already seeking other dogs.

Quickly, just in case anyone should notice her, she slipped behind the statue.

For four days she had searched with her fingers, only to be disappointed.

But today to her delight there was a folded piece of paper and in case anyone was watching her, she slipped it into her handbag.

Then she went to the other side of the Square where there was a seat. Bracken followed her when she called him and an attractive little terrier came with him.

Flavia sat down on the seat and looked around to make sure she was not being observed.

Then she took the piece of paper from her handbag and opened it.

"*The Grosvenor Chapel at eleven-thirty. Urgent.*"

That was all that was written, but she felt her heart jump.

The chase was on!

Although it was rather frightening in some ways, the excitement made her feel that she was back in action.

This in itself was most satisfactory and because she was so used to rising early in the country, even if she was late going to bed, she was usually downstairs before nine.

It was now only ten o'clock so there was plenty of time for her to go to the Grosvenor Chapel.

Even so, she looked at her watch a dozen times and it seemed to be going slower than it had ever gone before.

She kept wondering what had happened.

She felt sure that the Earl would not have sent for her unless he had something vitally important to tell her.

And she was trying to guess what it could be.

She wondered if he had found some subtle way of protecting them from her father's and Lord Carlsby's plot.

One thought had occurred to her only last night.

As the Earl did not want to marry her, he might easily become involved with or even marry someone else.

If he was entranced – as the Prince of Wales was – with someone as enchanting as Lillie Langtry, it would be impossible for her father and Lord Carlsby to involve him with her.

The plot would then grind to an abrupt standstill.

She suspected that being so good-looking the Earl must have had many *affaires-de-coeur*, as others did.

They were spoken of in front of her only with bated breath, but she and her father talked about them openly and it had inevitably started with the Prince of Wales.

"Is it really true, Papa," Flavia had asked, "that the Prince has had a great number of *affaires-de-coeur* with beautiful ladies, not only in London but in Paris?"

"Now who has been talking to you?" he asked.

"I was actually listening to something said to Mama when they did not think I was listening."

Her father had been amused.

"It's a great mistake for you to listen to gossip, but in this instance it would be stupid to try to keep the truth from you. Yes, the Prince of Wales has had many love affairs and it would be silly for me to pretend he is faithful to the Princess."

"Does she mind?" Flavia asked naively.

"If she does, she is clever enough to make it clear, as far as the outside world is concerned, that she and her husband are extremely happy with each other."

Lord Linwood had paused before he said positively,

"In public they appear to be a contented and happy couple."

"But the Princess must mind, if she loves him – "

"The Prince of Wales always treats her with great courtesy and insists on her receiving it from everyone else. What he does in private is not discussed at Marlborough House."

This was before the Prince had met Mrs. Langtry and Flavia had heard her father and his friends saying with astonishment that Princess Alexandra had accepted her.

This meant she was invited to Marlborough House and the Social world had followed Princess Alexandra's lead and opened their doors to her.

As Flavia had seen on the night of her dinner party, the Prince was very much in love.

Yet she had heard one of the ladies when they were in the drawing room saying that she had so enjoyed a party that had taken place at Marlborough House.

"His Royal Highness always thinks of something amusing to entertain us," she had said, "and that evening I think everyone was laughing from the moment they arrived until the moment they left."

Flavia longed to ask if Princess Alexandra was laughing too and almost as if the lady read her thoughts, she said,

"When we were just leaving, I heard Her Royal Highness saying to Mrs. Langtry, 'I do hope you will come again, as when you are here, His Royal Highness is always in such a great jovial mood and everyone finds the party entrancing'."

Flavia thought over what she had heard.

She wondered if perhaps the Earl had followed the Prince of Wales's example.

Was he indeed having a love affair with someone as beautiful as Mrs. Langtry?

If he was, it would be completely impossible for her father and Lord Carlsby to catch him out with her and claim that he had ruined her reputation.

It was just a thought.

Yet, she knew that if it was the end of this strange drama, she would in a way be relieved.

At the same time she would miss the excitement of wondering what could happen next or how she and the Earl could defeat the two of them, who were determined to lock them together in Holy Matrimony.

She took Bracken back to the house.

Then she spent some time choosing a pretty hat to go with the dress she was wearing.

When finally she was ready, it was fifteen minutes past eleven.

She needed to find someone to escort her to South Audley Street and it was safe to say that she was going there directly as she had done earlier.

She therefore approached Mrs. Shepherd,

"I am only going to the chemist to buy some more scent, so I will take Molly with me again. She so enjoyed coming with me the other morning that I felt I must take her again for old times' sake."

"You're very kind and considerate, Miss Flavia," Mrs. Shepherd said, "which be more than I could say for most young women of your age. All they thinks about is how they can doll themselves up for the dancing."

"I think you are being unkind, but, as you know, Molly has been with us longer, I think, than anyone else, and I don't want her to feel that she is too old for whatever we are doing now."

"She'll be very happy to go with you, Miss Flavia, and so would any of the others. But as you says yourself, Molly be getting old and you mustn't take her too far."

"Only to the chemist and this afternoon unless I get an invitation to tea with anyone, I would like Betty to come with me and we'll take Bracken for a walk in Hyde Park."

Mrs. Shepherd smiled.

"That's a good idea and what you needs be plenty of exercise. You were late this morning setting off for your ride and came back quicker than I expected."

Flavia could not say she had been disappointed as there was no sign of the Earl in Rotten Row.

There were just the same people she had seen every day and some had been at the party last night. She had therefore galloped with the groom behind her several times up and down the Row and then returned home.

Now she was feeling excited because the 'game' had started again.

She wondered what the Earl would have to tell her.

Holding Bracken's lead and walking very slowly as Molly could not hurry, they then turned into South Audley Street.

The chemist's shop was halfway down on the right hand side.

"I want you to go and ask for the scent I always use," Flavia said to Molly. "If he does not have it, tell him to order it for me."

She paused for breath before she added,

"I will leave Bracken with you while I run to the Post Office with a letter I have to send. I will not be long, but in case they keep me waiting sit down inside the shop – there is always a chair – and wait until I reappear."

"That's all right then, miss," said Molly, "I knows exactly what you want. Don't you hurry yourself too much as it's so hot."

Flavia saw Molly go into the chemists and then she walked as quickly as she could to Grosvenor Chapel.

The door was open as it always was and she saw as she peeped inside that there were three people praying in various pews.

Then, as she hurried upstairs to the Gallery, she was frightened in case there were worshippers there as well.

Much to her relief, however, there was only the Earl sitting where he had been before.

She moved quickly towards him, but he did not rise and she sat down beside him.

"I thought you had forgotten about me," she began.

"You can be quite certain I have not," he replied. "But I had no news to tell you until yesterday."

"What happened then?" Flavia asked breathlessly.

"Your father and Lord Carlsby have been extremely shrewd and have done something we did not expect."

"What is that?" Flavia asked.

"Your father suggested to Her Majesty that, as you have been such an amazing success since you appeared in London and everyone is now talking about your beauty, he thought it essential you should marry as soon as possible."

Flavia gave a gasp and stared at the Earl.

"Did Papa really say that to the Queen?"

"He did – and what is more, he suggested that Her Majesty would understand that I was definitely the most eligible bachelor in London at this moment and begged her help in drawing us together."

"I don't believe it!" Flavia exclaimed. "Surely my Papa cannot *really* have said that to Her Majesty."

"That is what Her Majesty told me. When I insisted it was nonsense and I had no wish to be married, she said she thought it would be good for me to have a wife. Also she understood that I was consorting with women like the Duchess of Manchester and that was something of which she most definitely disapproved."

"What did you say to her?"

"What could I say? I said I had no wish to marry anyone at the moment, and if I did, it must be someone I loved who would share the same interests as I have."

There was a pause and as his eyes twinkled, he added,

"I must now be honest and tell you that I said I was looking for someone just like Her Majesty when she was young!"

Flavia laughed because she could not help it.

Then she rapidly covered her lips with her hand in case she was overheard.

"That was very quick of you," she whispered.

"It is almost true. After all she is an intelligent woman and Lord Melbourne taught her so much when she was young that she is so different from the brainless young women who are pushed upon me at every ball."

"I wondered why you were not at the Duchess of Bedford's last night," Flavia commented.

"Do you mean you missed me, Flavia?"

"Of course I did. I find our dangerous situation, even though it is frightening, far more interesting than the conversation of the men who danced with me."

"You must have enjoyed the compliments they paid you. How many proposals of marriage have you had?"

Flavia answered him without thinking,

"Two, as it so happens, and one in the offing. But I would rather die than marry any of them."

"Why, what is wrong?"

"They are young and know little about anything except sport. And I should undoubtedly find them boring before the honeymoon was over."

"It's exactly how I would feel," the Earl exclaimed. "Now you will understand why I have no wish to marry, whatever the Queen or anyone else says."

"Could she hurt you in any way if you reject her advice?" Flavia asked him after a moment.

"She could make things very difficult for me and that of course is what your father and Lord Carlsby desire."

"In other words, either you marry me or you are no longer persona grata at Windsor Castle!"

"Exactly. Therefore we have to think of something brilliant as an answer."

Flavia was silent for a moment and then she said,

"I was actually thinking today that perhaps you had found someone who thrilled you in the same way that Mrs. Langtry thrills the Prince. If you were as much in love as they are, it would be impossible for Papa or Lord Carlsby to try to force you to marry me."

"That is certainly an idea, but at present I am not particularly attracted by anyone and I have no wish to go looking for more trouble than I am in already."

"You mean that, if the lady is married, her husband might take action against you?"

"Right again! It would certainly be a case of 'out of the frying pan and into the fire'!"

Flavia wanted to laugh and had great difficulty in preventing herself from doing so.

Then she asked in a different voice,

"What *can* we do?"

"I was hoping you would have an idea, Flavia. I don't want to frighten you, but I think it is only a question of time before the Queen orders your father to bring you to Windsor Castle."

"You mean Her Majesty will tell me outright that I have to marry you?" Flavia asked incredulously.

"She may do, I wouldn't put it past her. If she gets an idea into her head, it is almost impossible to push it out again."

There was silence and then Flavia murmured,

"You mean she really might order us to marry each other. If you refuse, it would ruin your career at Court."

"I was thinking," the Earl replied, "that one way I could circumvent them would be to go abroad. There are still parts of the world I have not seen and I always enjoy travelling."

"It's unfair that you can be so lucky. You can slip off quite happily and no one would think it strange, but you can imagine the hue and cry if I did such a thing."

He did not speak and after a moment she added,

"That is exactly what I would love to do. You will not believe it, but I do find London and the Season rather disenchanting. It has been exciting because you and I are attempting to prevent Papa and Lord Carlsby having their way. But now that the Queen has joined in, it may be more threatening than we had anticipated."

"It may not be as bad as I fear, but I thought you should know what was happening."

"Of course I have to know. You could not be so unkind as to leave me out. And if you just disappeared, I should find it intolerable to go on listening to all those silly and tedious young men!"

The Earl looked pensive for a moment,

"I thought when we first met, Flavia, the one thing you wanted was for me to ignore you and for us never to speak to each other again."

"That is what I wanted at first, but now I find it very disappointing when there is no message from you. I discovered that the fight we are having with Papa and Lord Carlsby is more intriguing than dancing round a ballroom every night with each partner exactly the same as the last."

"That is exactly what I have always felt," the Earl said. "I think really the wisest course we can now take is to sit tight and wait and see what happens."

Flavia looked at him wide-eyed.

"Do you really mean that? What will you do if the Queen orders you to marry me?"

"She will not do that in so many words, but she will make it very clear that it is her wish, and, of course, your father's, who she greatly respects, that we should be joined together. It will be very difficult for us to refuse when she offers us her blessing."

There was a note of sarcasm in his voice as he spoke the last words.

Then Flavia cried,

"Whatever happens neither of us must marry unless we are true to our convictions that we have to be wildly in love!"

"That is just what I am trying to say, Flavia. But being 'wildly in love' as you so elegantly put it, does not come naturally. As you grow older, you will find that most times one is disillusioned far too quickly and what one at first thought of as love becomes as dull and depressing as you found with your dancing partners last night."

"Now you are trying to disillusion *me*, but I have believed all my life that I would find the real love which comes from my heart and my soul. Once I found Prince Charming, we would live happily ever after!"

The Earl smiled.

"Go on believing it. It would be a great mistake for you to become disenchanted and an even greater mistake if you married someone and found out the truth once the ring was on your finger."

"That is what I am afraid of, but I pray and pray that one day someone will love me with his heart and soul and I will love him in the same way. Then we will really be happy."

She spoke very softly and, as she finished speaking, the Earl put his hand over hers.

"Then go on praying, Flavia, and somehow we will ensure that you find what you are seeking."

"And I hope you will find the same."

For a moment they sat in silence, his hand covering hers.

Then she asked in an agitated voice,

"What is the time? How long have I been here?"

The Earl looked at his watch.

"It's nearly a quarter to twelve."

"I have left my old maid at the chemist and she will wonder what has happened to me."

She picked up her handbag which was beside her.

"Promise me you will let me know what happens," she urged. "I will look every day to see if there is another message."

"I will let you know everything," the Earl replied. "Actually I am going down to Windsor Castle this very afternoon."

"Then you will not be at the dance tonight. I am sure you must have been invited to it as it is being given by one of the close friends of Mr. Disraeli."

"Her Majesty has sent for me and who can be brave enough to refuse a Royal command?"

"No, I understand you must be at Windsor Castle with her, but do find out what they are now planning and let me know as soon as you can."

"I promise you I will, Flavia. I am finding it as difficult as you are to think of a reasonable answer to Her Majesty."

"Reasonable! Nothing is reasonable if it is forced upon people when they don't want it."

"I agree with you, but don't be frightened. If the worst comes to the worst, then I can always sail off to some strange land I have not yet visited. Then while I am away everyone will forget about my very existence."

"How can you possibly do so when you have horses running at Ascot and you will surely then be planning an unusual event for the autumn?"

The Earl smiled.

"Well, I was thinking of a new and challenging steeplechase."

"I might have guessed it. Papa has told me you have a Racecourse on your estate and I am sure you are training your horses to win at Goodwood and all the other Classics."

"You must be reading my thoughts, Flavia."

"I really must go," she asserted, "at the same time please don't forget me and I will be longing to hear if it comes down to you either having to leave the country or facing the music."

"What about your side of the problem, Flavia? We have not even discussed it yet."

"I was just wondering," she replied after a moment, "whether I should indeed marry someone I don't yet know or meekly obey Her Majesty's command to marry *you*."

She was teasing the Earl and he was aware of it.

His eyes were twinkling as he answered her,

"You can always close your eyes and take a lucky dip to see which name comes out of the hat first."

"Perhaps I will try it. Now goodbye, and please, please remember that I am waiting to hear from you."

Flavia slipped away as she spoke.

The Earl, who had risen, sat down again.

He was thinking as he heard her footsteps down the stairs that she was surely the prettiest and definitely the most interesting young woman he had met for years.

Then, as if there was no escape, he could hear the Queen's stringent voice telling him what he had to do.

Flavia hurried back to the chemist afraid that Molly would be wondering what had kept her.

However, she found that the old maid was perfectly happy, inspecting a whole array of different scents that the chemist had laid out on the counter in front of her.

"I'm sorry if I have been too long, Molly, but I met an old friend and we started talking."

"That'll be all right, miss. I were just wondering which of these scents you'd prefer. Mr. Coombes tells me that your favourite be out of fashion now."

Mr. Coombes was the chemist and Flavia smiled at him.

"Is that true? I always thought it a very nice scent."

"If you try one of the new ones, miss, you'll find them much improved. It's because, although I shouldn't be saying so, they come from France."

"I have heard that French scents are now the very best, but my mother always felt she was being unpatriotic if she bought one."

"Well, miss, you try this one," Mr. Coombes said, putting the bottle into her hand. "It's the best one I have and every young man who dances with you will tell you the same."

Flavia took his advice and paid for the scent, which she was sure would be very romantic.

Then, as she and Molly walked on home, she was thinking of how excellent it would be to see the Earl again.

What a grave problem they shared between them in making up their minds over what they should do!

'He is so clever and I am sure that he will think of something,' Flavia told herself.

It was only as she was nearly home that she realised she no longer disliked the Earl as she had at first.

Nor did she think him as stuck-up and conceited as she had expected him to be.

He had been human and understanding – and not in the least theatrical or disagreeable about the position they were now in.

'I have a feeling he will find a way out,' Flavia told herself and there was no need, as he had said, for her to be frightened.

However, she thought it shrewd and at the same time annoying of her father to have asked the Queen to interfere in what was their very private and personal affair.

But by doing so, he had made it extremely difficult for the Earl.

He had, of course, done that deliberately and it was equally difficult for her and she had no idea what she could do now.

It was all very well for the Earl to know that he could run away to some distant and obscure place and he was undoubtedly being honest in saying he would enjoy it much more than the London Season.

But then he would be running away from his own responsibilities at home.

Although he had not said so, she felt he was well aware that his great possessions needed his presence as well as his interest in them.

Whichever way she looked at it, Flavia found the situation more and more difficult – and indeed much more upsetting than she had anticipated.

How could she have guessed that her father would ask for the Queen's help in getting rid of the Earl and, of course, because he was so grand and so rich, her father would welcome him as a son-in-law.

Papa doubtless assumed that she would be happy with him and she was sure he truly wanted that because he loved her.

'How then could I possibly be happy,' Flavia asked herself angrily, 'with a man who was forced to marry me when he did not want to? A man who was accepting me as his wife merely because it was a Royal command.'

Then once again she thought the only alternative where she was concerned was to marry someone else.

But who?

She thought of the men she had met since she came to London.

Of the two who had said they wanted to marry her, although she had not given them the least encouragement, and she knew, as she had said to the Earl, she would rather die than marry either of them.

'They are stupid,' she thought, 'and have had no experience of life in any other part of the world, as Papa and the Earl have.'

As she drew in her breath, she wondered what it would be like to travel with the Earl, to visit one of the strange places where he, on his travels, had already been.

She suddenly had a strange feeling that it might be wonderful!

CHAPTER SEVEN

At the ball that evening Flavia received her third proposal of marriage.

It was her own fault that the man reached such a climax, as she was not attending to what he was saying.

She was thinking of Windsor Castle and the Earl.

Then, as they danced out of the ballroom and into a quiet conservatory, the gentleman who still had an arm round her waist, piped up,

"Promise you will marry me, Flavia. I want you more than I have ever wanted anyone before. I know I will make you happy."

It was difficult for Flavia to explain to him that she had no wish to marry anyone – not until she loved a man beyond peradventure and she did not love *him*.

"I will make you love me," he persisted.

Flavia shook her head.

"Love does not happen like this. You have to love a person instinctively while your vibrations touch his."

She did not know why she was explaining this to him, except that in a way she was explaining it to herself.

However, he said firmly when she was going home,

"I will be seeing you again as soon as I can and I will not give up hoping."

He had spoken almost in a whisper so that only she could hear him.

But her Aunt Edith, who had chaperoned her to the ball because her father could not manage to be with her that evening, asked,

"What has this Richard just said to you? I may be wrong, but I feel he is very much in love with you."

Flavia smiled.

"I think many people believe they are in love when they are dancing to a vibrant band as we had this evening – but when they wake up in the morning and it is not there, they feel very different."

Her aunt looked at her as if she thought she was speaking strangely, but she did not argue.

She dropped Flavia off at Grosvenor Square and, as there were still three others with them in the carriage, there was no possibility of an intimate conversation.

Flavia found out from the night-footman that her father had already returned home and gone to bed early, saying he was tired.

"I will be careful not to wake him," she cautioned.

But she was glad that her father was back and not staying the night at Windsor Castle.

However, she found an unexpected note from him lying on her bed.

She opened it, guessing what it contained before she read,

"My dear Flavia,

I am sorry to be late, but I have exciting news for you. Her Majesty wishes to meet you tomorrow. Therefore don't go riding as we will leave fairly early for luncheon at Windsor.

Bless you and sleep well.

Your loving father."

Flavia read the note through twice.

She knew it was just as she expected and what the Earl had warned her was about to happen.

It was now when she saw it written down in black and white that she began to feel really apprehensive.

Was there any way either of them could escape?

Or was the Earl just being over-optimistic in saying he would think of something?

There was no answer to these questions.

She expected to lie awake ruminating about her predicament, but she was more tired than she realised and fell asleep almost immediately.

*

She woke when her maid called her and she had slept peacefully without dreaming.

"Breakfast's at nine o'clock, Miss Flavia," the maid said. "His Lordship says you'll be leaving soon after ten."

She dressed quickly in one of her prettiest gowns, as she knew she must look her best for her father.

Whatever the difficulties that lay ahead, she must be careful not to spoil her father's relationship with the Queen. He was so proud of being Her Majesty's confidant and it made up in some degree for the loss of her mother.

She looked at herself in the mirror when she was finally dressed.

Then she wondered if she should, for her father's sake, agree to marry the Earl even if he did not wish to marry her.

'I love Papa and I know he loves me,' she said to herself, 'but equally, he is no way entitled and nor is Lord Carlsby to choose a husband for me – especially someone who does not wish to marry me.'

When she went down to breakfast, her father was already there.

"Did you enjoy yourself last night?" he asked as she kissed him.

"I missed you Papa, and to tell the truth it was a very boring party, even though they had the best band and the supper was delicious."

"Then what was wrong, my dear?"

"You can guess the answer to that," replied Flavia.

She sat down at the breakfast-table.

"You mean the men bored you?" her father asked.

"They were much worse than usual and when I was thinking of something else, I had another proposal."

"Which I presume you refused,"

"Yes, of course," Flavia answered. "As you well know, Papa, I have no wish to marry anyone."

Lord Linwood pressed his lips together, but he did not say anything.

Almost as soon as they had finished breakfast, they started off for Windsor Castle.

It was a beautiful sunny day and so there was no particular need to hurry.

Flavia would have enjoyed the drive if she had not known the reason for the invitation.

When they arrived at Windsor Castle, she thought it looked very impressive, in fact just as she had expected it to be.

They were met by an equerry who told them that he would inform Her Majesty of their arrival.

It had been arranged beforehand that they should have luncheon with Lord Carlsby and some other courtiers.

"Will Her Majesty be having luncheon in her own apartments?" Lord Linwood asked.

The equerry smiled.

"Yes. As you know, Her Majesty dislikes large parties unless they are absolutely unavoidable. We have quite a number of Her Majesty's Royal relations staying in the Castle at the moment."

There was a slight frown on Lord Linwood's brow.

Flavia sensed he was worried that his plan might have to be postponed and she was half-afraid that the Earl might not turn up at the last moment and that would make her position even more difficult than it was already.

So she felt a sudden excitement and sense of relief at the sight of the Earl striding towards her.

He shook her hand and pressed it.

She knew then that he was still confident he could deal with the situation.

Her father and Lord Carlsby were being careful and they did not want to make Flavia or the Earl for that matter, aware that anything unusual was likely to happen.

Flavia found herself seated at luncheon next to two elderly Statesmen and the Earl was at the other end of the table between two ancient Ladies-in-Waiting.

Flavia felt that the whole scenario was something they would laugh about later – if the situation was not now so critical that it became impossible for them to laugh at anything.

Fortunately, the Statesmen were only too anxious to tell Flavia about Windsor Castle and the significant part it had played in the history of England.

"It surprises me," one of them said, "that you have never been here before."

"I have been living in the country," Flavia replied, "and, as I was in deep mourning for a year, I have only just been allowed to come to London."

"Well, you have certainly been a sensation since you appeared," the Statesman declared. "I am always being told by my wife and daughter what a success you are and now I have seen you I am not surprised."

Flavia smiled at him.

"That is very kind of you. You must tell Papa that you approve of me. This is my first visit to the Castle and I am sure he is afraid I will do something outrageous that would let him down!"

The Statesman laughed.

"I am sure you would never do anything like that. As I expect you know, Lord Linwood is a great help and comfort to Her Majesty."

"He is very proud to be and she certainly needs his guidance in the present difficult situation in Europe and I am not surprised that Her Majesty is grateful."

"Now you must not worry your pretty head about such issues. All you should worry about are the charming young gentlemen who want to dance with you and who I am sure are waiting to ask you to spend the rest of your life with them."

"What I want to do with my life is to see something of the world and to meet a great number of different people before I settle down with a husband and a large family."

The Statesman chuckled.

"Well, that is frank at any rate. I only hope you will be allowed to enjoy yourself as you wish to do."

He glanced up the table at the Earl as he spoke and Flavia had a suspicion that he had some idea of what had been taking place behind closed doors.

When luncheon was finished, and it did not take as long as Flavia expected, her father came to her side to say,

"Her Majesty the Queen has most graciously said she now wishes to meet you and I am to take you into her private apartments."

"How kind of her. I suppose you must sometimes have spoken to Her Majesty about me, Papa."

"I have talked about you a great deal. Her Majesty is delighted that you have been such a success since you arrived in London."

Flavia did not answer.

Then, as they started to walk to the door, she asked,

"Will Her Majesty be seeing you and me alone, or will there be anyone else present?"

She sensed that her father did not want to answer that question.

They walked on silently before he responded,

"I think we must wait until we get there before I can tell you exactly what is likely to happen."

Flavia drew in her breath.

Now the moment had actually arrived, she had to admit that she was feeling frightened.

It was all very well for the Earl to say he would think of some way to save them both.

Yet she was quite sure that it would be impossible for either of them to refuse to obey the Queen.

Even if she only expressed a wish, it was equivalent to a Royal command.

The Earl, she was increasingly convinced, had been overconfident in what was now a more or less impossible situation.

While she was ruminating, she and her father were moving through the long narrow passages, often described as the 'Windsor rabbit warren'.

At last, after walking what seemed an extremely long way from the dining room, they now entered what she reckoned must be Her Majesty's private apartments.

There were several equerries to greet them and they were shown into an anteroom and found that the Earl was already there.

He smiled at Flavia.

She longed to ask him if he had found the solution he had promised her – or whether they were to go in like sheep to the slaughter with nothing to protect or aid them.

When they reached the Earl's side, Flavia knew that her father was deliberately taking her to be next to him.

There were others there in the room – two Ladies-in-Waiting, several equerries and, not surprisingly, Lord Carlsby.

"I was just wondering how your horses are doing," Lord Linwood addressed the Earl.

Flavia realised he was trying to make it seem quite ordinary that they were both there without any of the other visitors who had been at the luncheon.

"I have hopes for at least three of them," the Earl replied.

"Then you must tell me which one is likely to win the big race tomorrow," Lord Linwood quizzed him.

He was talking quite casually, as if this was not a particularly important occasion.

Flavia felt a sudden impulse to turn and run away.

She was quite certain this had all been planned by her father and Lord Carlsby down to the minutest detail.

It would be absolutely impossible for either her or the Earl to gainsay the Queen or even protest at anything she suggested.

Then as she looked at the Earl almost beseechingly, she had the feeling that he was telling her without words not to be afraid.

She looked into his eyes and knew that he was quite certain that he could cope with all that lay ahead.

'I only hope you are right,' she wanted to say.

Then an equerry opened the door and announced,

"Her Majesty the Queen has graciously consented to receive the Honourable Miss Flavia Linwood and the Earl of Haugton."

Now that the moment had actually arrived, Flavia drew in her breath, not only in fear but also in surprise.

She had never for a single moment dreamt that the Queen would see her alone with the Earl.

She had expected at least her father would be there to present her in person, as he had always wanted to do.

As she stood irresolute, the Earl put out his hand.

Without even thinking, she slipped her fingers into it.

Lord Linwood bent forward as if to speak to his daughter, but the Earl moved her quickly across the room and through the door where the equerry was standing.

As he led them down a passage, the equerry said,

"Her Majesty commands that, as it is a nice day and the sun is shining, she would like to speak to you both in the garden."

Flavia was aware that the Earl raised his eyebrows and then he pressed her fingers as if to warn her not to say anything.

They walked down a small staircase and then there was an open door leading into the garden.

Standing just outside with the sun on her face was Her Majesty the Queen.

The Earl bowed.

"I know Vincent," the Queen said, "how much you enjoy the fresh air and the sunshine. Therefore I thought we would have a little talk here rather than in my room."

"Your Majesty thinks of everything," replied the Earl, "and may I present Miss Flavia Linwood, who I know you have heard about from her father."

The Queen put out her hand and Flavia sank down in a low and graceful curtsy.

"I have heard a great deal about Miss Linwood and all, I may say, to her advantage. Now come along and sit on my favourite bench and look at my very special view of the Great Park."

The Earl had released Flavia's hand as he presented her.

Now he made a step forward to offer the Queen his arm.

As he did so, Flavia saw to her intense surprise a rough-looking man appear over the stone wall just ahead of them.

He held a rifle in his hand and then he raised it to his shoulder.

Before she could utter any warning, the Earl gave a loud exclamation and flung himself in front of the Queen.

The man who was about to shoot, hesitated.

Then just as he raised his rifle again as if to shoot directly at the Earl, Flavia realised what was happening.

She gave a scream.

As the Earl was now standing in front of the Queen, she threw herself at him, throwing out both her arms, so that her back was protecting him from the gunman.

Then, as she waited for the sound of the shot, it came not from the gunman facing them but from behind him.

The bullet must have hit the gunman in the back.

As his rifle exploded harmlessly into the air, he fell down onto the ground behind the stone wall.

The noise of the two rifle shots seemed deafening.

Next, the garden door opened behind them.

Equerries and servants poured through.

Shouting at the top of their voices, they surrounded the Queen.

Despite the dastardly attempt to murder her, Her Majesty was surprisingly calm.

As they all hurried back into the Castle, the Earl reached out and took Flavia's hand in his.

She did not speak.

Her heart was beating tumultuously in her breast.

She knew that not only the Queen but she and the Earl had escaped sudden death by what seemed a miracle.

Sentries were now running from the lower part of the garden to where the gunman had fallen, shot down by one of the Queen's alert security guards, who had seen the man acting suspiciously and then acted decisively.

But the Earl now holding firmly onto Flavia's hand, drew her behind the people surrounding the Queen.

Hurrying her back into safety, they passed through the garden door and down the passage, the Earl and Flavia following behind them.

Then suddenly, much to Flavia's surprise, the Earl stopped and opened a door just to the side of them.

Before she realised what was happening, he pulled her through it and into a small sitting room.

It was empty.

The Earl closed the door behind them.

Again to her astonishment, he locked it and then he turned round to look at her.

She was still feeling as if her heart was beating so violently it might burst through her breast.

Her face was pale but very lovely, as she looked up at him.

"You saved – Her Majesty," she managed to stutter in a soft hesitating voice.

"And *you* saved me, Flavia. I want to thank you, and there is only one way I feel I can do so adequately."

She felt his arms go round her as he spoke.

Then his lips were on hers, holding her so closely against his chest it was just impossible to move and almost impossible to breathe.

As he kissed her, she felt a strange and wonderful sensation sweep through her entire being.

It was something she had never known or imagined before.

Yet she knew it was exactly what she had always wanted and believed she would never find.

The Earl kissed her and went on kissing her until she felt as if her whole body had melted into his and she was part of him.

Then he raised his head.

"Now," he said and his voice was very deep and a little unsteady, "tell me what you feel about me."

"I love – you," Flavia murmured. "I did not know – that love could be so wonderful."

"Nor did I, my darling, I am asking myself how it is possible you can make me feel like this."

She did not answer him, but he gazed deeply into her eyes as he went on,

"I have loved you for a good long time, but I fought against it, because I knew you did not love me and had no wish to marry me. But I think, my darling, *we now know the answer to our problem*."

Without waiting for her reply, he was kissing her again.

Kissing her wildly, demandingly, passionately, as if he was forcing her to tell him that her love was as strong as his.

"I love you, Flavia."

"And – I love you, Vincent."

When they could speak, that was all they could whisper to each other.

At last the Earl sighed,

"Her Majesty was going to ask us to marry each other, but we have solved the problem for ourselves!"

Flavia smiled and then she asked the Earl,

"Are you quite certain that is what you want?"

"I loved you as soon as I first saw you," the Earl answered, "but I fought hard against it, being afraid that however much I tried, I could never make you love me."

"I did not know – that love could be so wonderful or – like this," Flavia whispered.

"This is only the beginning, my precious. I think we will be very very happy."

"Papa and Lord Carlsby wanted to get rid of you," Flavia murmured, "because they thought you were a bad influence on the Queen – they at least will be delighted!"

The Earl was still and she asked him,

"What are you thinking?"

"I was just thinking how boring it will be to keep hearing that it was *their* idea and how clever *they* have been to know before we did ourselves that we loved each other!"

Flavia gave a little cry.

"Of course they will say it and a great deal more!" she exclaimed. "Oh, must we listen to all that? It might spoil everything we are feeling now."

"Nothing could ever spoil this wonderful love, but you are quite right to ask why we should listen to them."

"How can we help doing so?" Flavia questioned.

"We are going to run away," cried the Earl, "and the quicker the better."

"What do you mean, Vincent?"

The Earl did not answer.

Taking her by the hand, he unlocked the door and drew her through it.

As he expected, the passage was empty.

The equerries had obviously taken the Queen back to her private apartments.

As he knew the Castle so well, the Earl started to run in the opposite direction pulling Flavia by the hand.

He moved so quickly that it was quite difficult for her to keep up with him.

As he reached a large door, he stopped suddenly.

Putting his arm round Flavia, he suggested,

"Now you must look pale and distressed – "

She had taken off her hat before luncheon because none of the ladies present were wearing hats.

She put her fair head against the Earl's shoulder, half closed her eyes, and he then put his arms around her as if he was supporting her from collapsing onto the floor.

"Will you tell Lord Linwood that his daughter is suffering from shock," he muttered to one of the assembled courtiers, "and I am taking her home."

"I have just heard there has been trouble outside in the garden," he replied. "Is Her Majesty all right?"

"I think that she too is suffering from shock – "

Then, as if he could not waste any more time, he passed through the outer door.

As he knew the way, in a very short time he found the chaise he had arrived in.

Everyone appeared to be hurrying backwards and forwards and no one seemed to notice them particularly.

The Earl took up the reins and his groom jumped into the seat behind.

As they drove off, Flavia cried,

"We have done it! We have got away! You are so clever!"

"We avoided what would be hours of talk as to who the man was and why he wanted to assassinate the Queen," the Earl replied. "I don't suppose they will come to any conclusion even if they talk until midnight!"

"I don't want to listen to them, but tell me where we are going, Vincent?"

"I have an idea that will save us from having to listen to them telling us that they have always known we were made for each other and it is entirely due to them that we have fallen in love. *We must escape!*"

"But how and where to?"

As he did not reply, she gave a sigh and asked him,

"Do you really love me enough, my darling Flavia, to run away with me here and now and so avoid all these tiresome diversions that could spoil our happiness?"

"What are you suggesting?"

The Earl thought for a moment,

"I am taking you back to Grosvenor Square and I want you then to pack up everything you will need for our honeymoon. We can easily buy anything you forget later."

"Where are we going?" Flavia asked. "What are you planning?"

"Just leave it to me. You will have to learn to love and obey me and I want you to start *now*!"

Flavia laughed.

"How could I have guessed you would love me?"

"I loved you from the first moment I saw you," the Earl affirmed. "But I had been, as you know, determined never to marry, and then, when I knew I wanted to marry *you*, you were intent on telling me how much you disliked me."

"But I soon found I wanted to be with you, Vincent, and I found everyone else a bore when I was not with you."

"That's a very good foundation on which to build our marriage," the Earl smiled.

Flavia looked at him.

"Can I not ask you how and where we are going to be married if we run away," she questioned him.

"I want you to leave that to me for a little longer. I have an idea and I rather suspect it will please you."

"You are being very mysterious, but I will be a very good and subservient wife-to-be and will not ask you any more questions!"

"There is one thing I do know and that as my wife you will be good for me in every way. That I promise you is something I have never said to any other woman."

"Of course I am very honoured and very surprised that you should say it to me, Vincent."

She was laughing and laid her cheek on his arm.

"This is the most exciting thing," she murmured softly, "that has ever happened to me."

"It will go on being exciting, Flavia, now and for the rest of our lives."

They reached Grosvenor Square in record time.

"I will be back as soon as I can," the Earl told her. "It's essential, as you well know, for us to be away before your father returns from Windsor Castle."

"I'll pack everything as quickly as I can."

Flavia jumped out of the carriage and even before the front door opened for her, the Earl had driven away.

She wondered where he was going and what he had in his mind.

However, she knew she must do as he said and ask questions later.

She had not been in her bedroom for long and was pulling clothes out of the wardrobe when Mrs. Shepherd appeared.

"I hears you was back, Miss Flavia," she said, "but it's sooner than we had expected. What are you doing with your clothes?"

"I am going to stay with friends in the country for a very special party and they are calling for me very shortly. Please get these packed just as quickly as you can. I must not keep them waiting."

If Mrs. Shepherd thought it was a bit strange, she was too well trained to say so. She merely called for the maids and they started to pack everything Flavia had pulled out of the wardrobe into her travelling cases.

As they did so, she just had time to write a note to her father to tell him that she was going away to stay with friends, and she would let him know as soon as she could when she would be returning.

'He will worry far more about the Queen than he will about me,' she reflected ruefully.

Then she told herself that she was acting wrongly in deceiving him.

'I must persuade Vincent to tell Papa where we are as soon as I know myself,' she mused. 'At the moment he is being so secretive.'

"I were hoping, miss, you'd tell us," Mrs. Shepherd was saying as Flavia finished writing the note to her father, "about Windsor Castle and what Her Majesty the Queen says to you."

"I am sure Papa will tell you all when he arrives," Flavia answered. "I am in too much of a hurry to think of anything but being ready for my friends. Otherwise they might go without me."

"I don't believe they'd do that, miss."

But Flavia was already rushing from the room and hurrying down the stairs, hoping that the carriage would be outside waiting for her.

Actually, the packing had taken much longer than she expected.

She had changed into a dress that was even prettier than the one she had worn to go to Windsor Castle – it was white as was expected of a *debutante* and was even more elaborate than a day dress, although not *décolletée* enough to be called an evening gown.

And it made her look even lovelier than she had at luncheon.

As she tidied her hair in the mirror, she thought the Earl would want to kiss her again and felt herself thrill at the memory of his fervent kisses, which she could still feel on her lips.

As a very last thought, she put her mother's pearl necklace round her neck and a bracelet to match it round her wrist.

As she reached the hall, she heard a footman open the front door and say,

"I'll tell Miss Flavia Your Lordship's here."

To her surprise, she saw the Earl was not waiting as she had expected in his chaise.

Instead he was in a closed carriage drawn by a pair of well-bred horses and her cases were piled onto the back.

As she stepped in, Barker asked,

"Shall I tell his Lordship where you've gone, Miss Flavia?"

"I have written this letter to my father. Please give it to him when he returns, Barker."

She saw the surprise on Barker's face and then the footman shut the door and sprang up beside the coachman.

As they drove off, the Earl pulled her close to him and kissed her.

They were long demanding kisses, almost as if he had been half-afraid she would not come at the last minute and he would lose her.

When at last she could speak, Flavia asked him,

"Where are we going, Vincent? You have not told me anything."

"We are going to be married and everything is now settled just as I planned it would be."

"What is settled and where are we being married?"

"I can tell you now," he said, "that I had hoped and hoped that you would agree willingly to marry me if you knew I truly loved you and wanted you. That the attempt to assassinate the Queen precipitated matters was just a *piece of luck* for me."

The Earl's arms tightened round her as he went on,

"We are being married, my darling, in the Chapel at Marlborough House. And the Best Man, in fact the only witness at our wedding, will be the Prince of Wales!"

Flavia stared at him.

"I don't believe it," she exclaimed.

"I felt it would be the answer to all our problems from those who tried to interfere with us and get the Queen to force us into matrimony. The Prince of Wales was only too delighted to be 'one up', as you might say, on Windsor Castle. He has arranged for his Chaplain to be waiting for us at his private Chapel and he will be there too."

For a moment, Flavia gasped and then she laughed.

"I cannot believe it's true. It's all too much like a story in a book and could not ever happen in real life."

"I assure you it's all happening, Flavia, and because we are running away and the Prince is well aware that your father and Lord Carlsby disapprove of him, he is lending us his yacht to take us on the first part of our honeymoon.

"After that we will decide whether we will go and visit the lands you have only read about in books or heard talked about by explorers."

Flavia gave a cry of delight.

But it was impossible to say any more because the Earl was kissing her again.

*

The little Chapel at Marlborough House was in the garden facing the Mall.

With a gesture Flavia thought extremely touching, the Prince of Wales had ordered flowers from the house to be brought into the Chapel.

There were six candles burning on the altar.

The Chaplain, wearing white and gold vestments, was waiting for them.

The Earl entered the Chapel first.

Flavia followed on the arm of the Prince of Wales.

The Service was short, but the Chaplain, who was an elderly man, read it with great sincerity.

It made Flavia feel as though every word spoken was blessed by God.

She felt as if the angels were singing overhead and that her beloved Mama was there in the Chapel praying for her future happiness.

When they knelt for the blessing, the ring, which she learnt later had belonged to the Earl's mother was now glittering on her finger.

When the Service finally ended, they did not go to Marlborough House but down to the Embankment.

The Prince of Wales's fine yacht, of which he was exceedingly proud, was waiting for them.

As soon as they came aboard and the Prince had drunk their health in champagne, they moved out into the mid-stream of the river.

As the Prince waved goodbye, Flavia slipped her arm through the Earl's.

"I cannot believe this is true," she sighed. "How can we have been married so quickly and so beautifully?"

Before he could reply, she went on,

"How could you think of anything so marvellous as to ask the Prince of Wales for his Private Chapel?"

The Earl smiled.

"I knew the Prince had always resented your father and Lord Carlsby knowing more about the affairs of State than he was allowed to know. He was therefore delighted for once to be 'first past the winning post', so to speak."

Flavia giggled, knowing this to be true.

"His mother," the Earl continued, "can hardly take the credit for marrying us off when he had already done so in his own Private Chapel at Marlborough House!"

His eyes twinkled as he finished,

"Then, to have lent us his own yacht, with which he is determined to astonish all the competitors at Cowes this year, will leave the Social world gasping."

"I do see, Vincent, it's all 'wheels within wheels'."

"The only thing that really does matter is that we are married and no one can take you away from me."

Their eyes met and it was impossible for either of them to speak.

Then, as the yacht moved on slowly down the river, they walked into the Saloon for dinner.

It was only as they were finishing a delicious meal that Flavia managed to murmur,

"I am feeling rather guilty about Papa. I will have to let him know we are married."

"I thought you would think that, my darling," the Earl replied. "As I felt the same, I asked the Prince to tell him all the details tomorrow morning."

"You have asked the Prince to tell him!"

Then Flavia laughed.

"Oh, I see how your mind is working! It will be a great delight to the Prince, as you have said, to be 'one up' on Papa and Lord Carlsby as well as on the Queen."

"Exactly, Flavia. You do see that he has achieved – with a wave of his hand – what they have been struggling for months to accomplish but to no avail."

Then they were both laughing.

"You are so clever, Vincent. That is what I love about you."

"Just as I love everything about you, from the soles of your feet to the top of your lovely head. Now you are mine, I will take very good care that not too many other men tell you how beautiful you are. I think the safest way to achieve that is by travelling to strange places where no one will be in the least impressed by you!"

Flavia laughed again.

"You are not frightening me, Vincent. You know as well as I do that we have to see your wonderful horse winning the Gold Cup at Ascot and I am sure you have a great responsibility for your estate and possessions."

The Earl smiled at Flavia tenderly.

"I knew you would think that, but sometimes we will sneak away to be on our own. And we must look after our own people and do our best, as the Queen is doing, to make England great."

Flavia leaned forward so that she could put her head against his shoulder.

"I love the way you think," she sighed. "It's so easy to talk to you because you understand what I am trying to say as no one else has ever done."

"I love and understand every little bit of you, from the thoughts behind your clever brain right down to your tiny toes that dance better than anyone else has ever done."

Flavia gave a cry.

"You say such lovely things to me and I am only scared that after all your talk about being afraid of being tied down and not wishing to be married, you will soon be bored with me and be looking for pastures new."

"I will not be doing that – for the simple reason we will never be bored with each other. We have so much to say that I doubt if we can complete it all in one lifetime. In fact I am almost certain this is just another life and we have lived so many together already."

"That is another subject I have a lot to say about!" Flavia asserted.

They were chuckling as they left the Saloon and went down to the Master Suite.

*

There were flowers in the room that had been sent with the compliments of the Prince of Wales.

And later that night as Flavia lay in the Earl's arms, she could smell the scent of roses and honeysuckle.

Because the Earl had not spoken for a few minutes, she whispered,

"Do you still love me, Vincent?"

"My darling, my sweet," he answered. "I love you a thousand times more than I did before I made you mine. And I will love you a thousand times more tomorrow and the day after."

"I was so frightened I might disappoint you."

The Earl pulled her closer to him.

"That is impossible, because everything about you is perfect and the most exciting thing I have ever done is to teach you about love."

"It was wonderful – for me," Flavia murmured.

"It will become even more wonderful as we get to know each other better. This is the beginning of a new life and a new world and I think you will find that every day we will grow closer and closer to each other."

Then he was kissing her again.

Kissing her at first gently, then more passionately.

The fire burning within them carried them both up towards the sky.

It surged through Flavia's mind that when she had seen the shooting star, she had believed it would bring her luck.

Now she realised that the shooting star had been the Earl himself all the time.

He had indeed *flashed* into her life and made her his completely.

As they touched the stars, the Gates of Paradise opened before them.

They walked in to find, as they had already done, the real love that comes from God and is God.

It is the sublime love all people seek and only a few are lucky enough to find.

"I love you, Vincent, I love you," Flavia whispered.

The Earl's voice was deep as he replied,

"I love, adore and worship you, my precious wife. You are perfect and no man could ever ask for more."